THE
NINTH
CIRCLE
Brendan Deneen

Praise For
★THE NINTH CIRCLE★

Brendan Deneen's debut novel, THE NINTH CIRCLE, tells the story of a young runaway who finds himself drawn into the strange, often dangerous and certainly bizarre world of a fantastical circus. Imaginative, dark, and surreal, this is one coming of age tale that will haunt you long after you turn the last page.

-Kristin Hannah, New York Times-bestselling author of
FIREFLY LANE

Surgically precise, irresistible, tragically cool, and jacked up with the smart-talk and surly attitudes of high school culture, Brendan Deneen's modern fantasy THE NINTH CIRCLE grabs the reader with a grappling hook and doesn't let go until the final page. Echoes of Bradbury reverberate between the lines - the master would have loved this. Very creepy and highly recommended!

-Jay Bonansinga, *New York Times***-bestselling co-author of** *THE WALKING DEAD: THE FALL OF THE GOVERNOR*

Ever want to run away to the circus? And what would that really be like? With the storytelling skills of a master, Brendan Deneen's THE NINTH CIRCLE summons the mythic yet very real tale of young Daniel, 16, and his escape from hell at home to something magical and amazing. Filled with moments that will have readers imagining the circus of their dreams and nightmares, THE NINTH CIRCLE holds a big-top mirror up to 'Dante's Inferno'. As readers watch Daniel become involved with classic circus archetypes - a clown, the ringmaster, the acrobat and even, yes, the geek - we follow Daniel and this traveling troupe that, with each Canto, goes deeper into the dark secrets of this strange circus. As if channeling a modern era Nightmare Alley or even Tod Browning's Freaks, THE NINTH CIRCLE is compelling reading, both haunting and totally unforgettable.

-Matthew Costello, bestselling and award-winning author of *RAGE* **and** *VACATION*

A surreal and unsettling tour of Hell through the eyes of a young man in the circus. THE NINTH CIRCLE is undeniably compelling, cant-look-away reading.

-Nate Kenyon, award-winning author of *DAY ONE* **and** *DIABLO: STORM OF LIGHT*

THE NINTH CIRCLE is a vibrant and assured coming of age tale, full of the fantastical, strange and grotesque. If cool, dark circuses and compelling characters are your thing, this is the book for you.

-Megan Chance, award-winning author of *BONE RIVER*

THE NINTH CIRCLE

Brendan Deneen

PERMUTED PLATINUM

Published by Permuted Press
109 International Drive, Suite 300
Franklin, TN 37067

Cover art by Dean Samed, Conzpiracy Digital Arts.

Follow us online:

Web: http://www.PermutedPress.com
Facebook: http://www.facebook.com/PermutedPress
Twitter: @PermutedPress

For Kim,
my inspiration from the start.

ACKNOWLEDGEMENTS

I started writing this novel in 1995, so there are many people to thank. Probably so many that I'm going to forget some, so I apologize in advance if you're reading this and thinking, "Where the hell is my thank you?!?" First and foremost, I want to thank my wife, Kim Field, for helping inspire this story way back in 1995. I'd also like to thank my two daughters, Eloise and Charlotte, for being constant inspirations, though I hope they don't read this book anytime soon. Thanks to my agent, Charlie Olsen, and my Permuted team, including Michael Wilson. Also, a thank you to Anthony Ziccardi. I'd also like to thank Richard Pine for his early interest in the book and for connecting me with Charlie. Thanks to my parents for always supporting and encouraging my creative endeavors. And finally, thanks to Katherine Dunn for writing GEEK LOVE. It's one of my all time favorite books. She's the reason I reached out to Richard, who connected me with Charlie, who connected me with Permuted. I guess there's a little bit of geek in all of us!

CANTO ONE

H igh school is Hell.
 I don't care if you're popular, nerdy, theatrical, sporty, political, admired, loved or hated. It sucks for everyone. The only difference is how you handle it. Are you a torturer or a victim? Do you give pain or do you receive it? Or are you one of the rare exceptions... like me... where you're ignored by both sinner and saint alike, both the blessed and the cursed? This social no man's land is an odd place to navigate, but it's exactly where I spend most of my days.

As the younger of two boys, I've made it my mission to fly under the radar. Most of the time, at school anyway, it works like a charm. By the time teachers or bullies figure out who I am, the school year's almost over. I'm not as lucky at home, where I'm the singular object of my older brother's aggression. At my house, he has raised torture to an art form. Just when I think he can't possibly think of a new way to inflict pain, he dreams up something that would impress a medieval prison guard.

Where are my parents during all of this? Good question. My father falls in love nightly with whatever bottle he's holding, while my mother loves... well, none of us know his name but we're all aware that he exists, even if no one says anything about it. Maybe my father has convinced himself that his wife isn't cheating.

Did I say high school is Hell? Maybe I meant life is Hell.

And today is no exception. Walking down the school hallway, minutes before the opening bell rings, the other kids stretch out in front of me like a weird, distorted forest. I weave among them quietly, cautious, hoping I don't disturb any of them. Today of all days, I want to stay under the radar.

But then I make my mistake.

I see her. Camilla. She's the only one. The only one at this whole damn school who means anything to me.

And she doesn't even know that I exist.

Sometimes, rarely, my ability to disappear in plain sight works against me.

But to my complete and utter surprise, she notices me as I nudge past her, and she smiles, and she says, "Hey Dan. Isn't today—?"

Even as her words are registering, I can see the impact approaching. Ben has never liked me, even way back in kindergarten. I feel like they were already a couple back then, and I just stood in the wings, invisible, forgotten, totally in love with a girl who didn't know my name. Or so I thought.

Ben slams me so hard into the lockers that I swear I hear my left arm snap. I let out a girlish scream and have to keep myself from crumbling to the dirty, foul-smelling carpet.

"Get lost, geek," he hisses into my face, and then he's gone, laughing with his jock friends, pulling Camilla along by her wrist. She gives me a pitying glance before she vanishes into the crowd, and I hate her for it.

As the bell rings and the other kids disperse into the various classrooms, I lean against the row of multicolored lockers and try to catch my breath. By the time I do, I'm the only one left in the hallway. I cradle my arm and fight back tears.

Did I mention it's my birthday? I'm sixteen. Yay me.

For some reason, my parents surprise me with tickets to the circus as soon as I get home from school. I've never expressed an interest in this kind of thing... I actually think circuses are kind of lame... so I have no idea where this is coming from. My brother is seriously pissed off that he has to go, too. He was supposed to have a date with some college girl and based on the way he looks at me as we all pile into the car—I'm going to pay for ruining his night.

On the way there, he hits me so hard in my already-hurt arm that I gasp and see stars. My parents sit in silence, unaware of the pain I'm in, or maybe they just don't give a shit.

Of all the freaks displayed behind glass cases in the corridor leading to the big top, she's the first one who really looks at me. And despite the shaggy beard covering her face, I immediately know she's a woman.

As I stare, she kneels and places her palm on the glass, her dark eyes working through me. My brother is already up ahead with my parents, passing through the canvas flap that leads into the circus. I smile at the Bearded Lady and then reluctantly turn away.

I hurry down the corridor after my family but steal a glance back at the sign on the top of her case: *Hairy Carrie*. Another kid stands in front of the glass now, blocking her from me.

In my rush to catch up, the rest of the freaks blur: a woman gift-wrapping herself with snakes; a mostly-naked man tattooed from bald head to toe; a lady who's just too fat; and some creature biting deep into the neck of a chicken, blood hitting hard against its face.

At the entrance to the big top, two proffered fists stop me. They belong to a skinny dude with too much makeup and a green satin and lace costume.

"Guess and win," he mumbles.

Instinctively, my right hand shoots out, forcing his left open. I'm rewarded with a cigarette-stained yellow palm. The other fist reveals a quarter, tails up.

"Better luck next time," he says, not even looking at me, and then he's gone. Music calls from between the canvas, drawing me in.

I catch my family's triangular shape hovering on nearby stairs. My brother stalks ahead of my parents, colorful lights dotting his body like a leopard. A Fortune Teller in a billowing robe moves among the slow-moving crowd, staring intently at dark palms, whispering the future.

I fix my eyes on the slanted glow of the aisle as the house lights begin to dim.

My family is already seated, coats off, as I force grudging knees to straighten. My brother kicks me in the shin to acknowledge I've been missed. I settle in between my father's large dark hands and my mother's angry stare.

"Glad you could make it," my father whispers sarcastically, the alcohol on his breath curling out like a lion's claws.

"Try to keep up next time," my mother scolds. My brother releases a cackle as the last of the lights fade.

A rumble of drums climaxes with the darkness, a spotlight illuminating a figure in the central ring. He's tall and narrow in a dark top hat and a blood-colored suit.

"Ladies and gentlemen... children of all ages..." his voice echoes, "Welcome to the circus!"

On cue, the lights and music erupt, and the Ringmaster vanishes.

"Faggot," my brother says as I clap.

In the farthest ring, one male and three female clowns roll over each other, squirting flowers, riding tiny bicycles, and intentionally messing with the other members of the troupe, much to their anger and the audience's delight.

In the center ring, a huge bald man with the name Kane on his massive belt buckle lifts a small car above his head, letting loose an audible snarl. My mother stares hard.

In the final ring, the Lion Tamer cracks his whip feverishly as his two assistants circle. He goes on to risk his obviously-prized hair by placing his entire head into the maw of a particularly drugged-looking lion.

And all the while, the acrobats twirl weightless above us. During one of their more spectacular runs of flips and catches, I stare for a long time and realize that one, a woman, is easily thirty years older than her partners. But she's flawless, just another part of the machine.

Below, a man shoots fire out of his mouth. Muscular, oiled women wave from within elephants' twisted trunks. Masked horses prance and jump. A man places a sword down his throat and then coughs it back up without batting an eye. Costumed dancers gyrate dramatically. Tinny, prerecorded music throbs in time with the acrobats' flips. And a retarded man limps after the animals with a shovel.

In what seems like no time at all, the music begins to fade and the performers dance and roll and lumber out of the rings one by one. My father bites down a yawn. Then the last of them, a clown I think, creeps away and the lights dwindle to a single line striking the dirt.

"Thank you, good night," the Ringmaster says from just outside the ring of light, then somewhere a switch flicks and all goes dark.

I was wrong earlier, when I said the circus was lame. It's not lame. It's awesome.

I keep my nose pressed against the window on the way home, watching my breath expand against the glass and recede into hollow rings of vapor. Traffic is bad. Everyone's quiet. My brother finds a safety pin on the floor and pokes it gently into my leg over and over again. I replace the pain with thoughts of spinning bodies, tiny people, painted faces, and a blood-red suit. Never a quitter, my brother pierces my thigh deeply and I emit a thin shriek, hitting my teeth against the glass. My mother looks back from the passenger seat into my wet eyes.

"Shh," she hisses through a circle of mouth. In the passing glare of headlights, she looks feral. I look down at my upturned palms.

When we finally pull up in front of our run-down apartment complex, I lean forward to see the dash: a little after midnight. My brother's eyes are shut tight. Even asleep he looks dangerous.

Later, in bed, I listen to our small apartment. My brother tosses violently on the other side of the room. Across the hall, my mother whispers into the phone with... whoever he is. And downstairs, my father sits mumbling and slamming a bottle against the tabletop.

I stare at the ceiling for hours and imagine the single beam of light hitting the dirt.

I walk out the front door of our complex at three-thirty in the morning. A few cars slow as they pass me but no one stops.

Finally, as the moon begins to disappear, I reach the hill where the circus took place. Without stopping for breath, I sprint up, my heart pounding against my ribs. At the top, nothing is left but litter and dirt. Even the chain link fence that had encircled the tents and trailers is gone.

Exhausted, I kneel and push my palms into the upturned earth.

After a moment, a shadow falls across my body. I turn and see eyes glimmering in the shadows.

"Hello there," the Ringmaster says, now wearing civilian clothes.

I stand up and look him in the face. "Um... hi," I mumble.

"Good thing we didn't leave with everyone else," he says.

A car approaches from the dark, the Bearded Lady behind the wheel.

"I want to go with you," I say, my voice foreign to my own ears.

Without answering, the Ringmaster nods and opens the rear door for me.

I look back at the fading lights of Boston. The engine idles quietly and a grey exhaust cloud washes over me. I turn my back on the city and get into the car. The Ringmaster slides into the passenger seat.

We drive slowly down the hill, away from the garbage-strewn clearing, silent.

CANTO TWO

~~~~~~

I wake from a dream of rain and candles.

A slice of sunlight beats against my face through a small window above me. It takes me a minute to realize that I'm lying on a cot, still fully clothed, nowhere near home. Yawning, I look around: old curtains covered with illustrations of balloons; half-open plywood door revealing a cramped bathroom; a mattress in the corner, blankets tucked haphazardly underneath.

Once outside, I'm surprised at how warm it is. The door swings shut with a tinny clank behind me. In the distant clearing, men and women labor with the big top, shouting curses and instructions. People mill about everywhere: in the shade of tents, running in and out of trailers, practicing flips and dances and falls. As I descend the steps, the Ringmaster divorces himself from the crowd and approaches me. Although I remain a step up, he still towers over me.

"Good afternoon," he says.

"Hey," I answer quietly.

A man with a ladder passes behind him. After another moment, the Ringmaster sits down next to me. I sit, too, and we watch the bustling activity for several minutes without a word.

"Where are we?" I finally ask.

"Providence," he answers, not looking at me.

A workman levels a large hammer just above a barely-submerged stake and then lets loose, smashing it into the resistant earth.

"I think I made a mistake," I say.

The Ringmaster looks at my profile. I keep my eyes from him and instead watch two male midgets practicing a stunt: handstand on the other's upwardly stretched palms. They fall, mount again, fall. The tents ruffle in the morning breeze.

"That's up to you," the Ringmaster says. "I'm sure your family is looking for you... the police... I was hoping you'd decide to stay on but maybe it would be best if—"

Another form withdraws itself from the crowd and approaches us. It's the Bearded Lady again, Hairy Carrie. She stands in front of us and doesn't say a word, just flashes a beautiful hair-encircled smile. Something about her eyes reminds me of Camilla.

"Morning, Alicia," the Ringmaster says at last, rising to greet her. "You remember Daniel from last night."

"Of course," she answers, turning her beard in my direction. "Though the only thing we got out of you before you passed out was your name."

Behind them, one of the Lion Tamer's Assistants struts past and disappears into a trailer. Alicia's eyes follow him for a moment and then she turns back to me.

"I remember you from yesterday," Hairy Carrie says to me, "When you were looking through the glass."

"Yeah, I... uh... it was my birthday."

Her blue-grey eyes reflect the sky. My stomach twists as she stares.

"Nice to see you again," she says, and with that she turns and merges back into the shuffling bodies. I notice for the first time that she's wearing overalls, and looks sexy in them.

"Whenever you're ready, I can make arrangements to get you back home," the Ringmaster says.

The workers continue to assemble the big top as the performers move among one another, talking and laughing. I catch a glimpse of Hairy Carrie as she vanishes into a trailer.

"Sorry," I finally answer. "I changed my mind again. I'd like to stay, if that's okay with you."

"Of course," he replies after a moment, smiling. "Like I said, it's totally up to you. You're not the first kid to run away to the circus... myself included. I'll make sure your presence here stays... quiet. Trust me... I know what it's like when you want to be left alone by the world. Come on. Let me give you a tour before everyone starts prepping for the show."

He leads me down the steps and into the fierce noise of the crowd.

CANTO THREE

A young woman with short hair comes running up to us as we make our way between trailers. She beams at the Ringmaster, clutching a cardboard box in her arms.

"Hi," she breathes, not looking at me. "We got the flyers you ordered. Micky's out putting them up. And I hear a lot of tickets already sold."

"Good," the Ringmaster says and rests his eyes on the box. The woman holds it up and removes the cover. Purple paper stares back, balloon-shaped and obscenely bright.

Come to the circus! the flyer screams. Where Fantasy Ends and Reality Begins!!!

The Ringmaster's face darkens as he reads the flyer.

"Celeste," he says quietly. "This is wrong. Reality is supposed to come first."

"Oh," she murmurs. "Oh, shit. Well, it's not my fault. I don't—"

"Find Micky. Tell him to take them all down."

"No one'll even notice. Can't we just..."

The Ringmaster stares at her from within the shadow of his top hat and her words trail away. She's a little overweight and not attractive. I fight back a nervous laugh at the silence.

"Now," the Ringmaster orders.

Celeste manages a feeble smile, then turns and heads back the way she'd come. The Ringmaster moves on. I walk quietly next to him. A midget with a five o'clock shadow passes us and stares without curiosity.

"That's Pluto," the Ringmaster says when the little man is out of sight. "He's the Lead Midget. His real name is Gerry but almost everyone goes by their stage names."

We reach the clearing where the big top is being assembled. The freak show corridor is already standing.

"That always goes up first," the Ringmaster says, following my gaze. "Some tradition. I can't remember why."

Across the clearing, a small crowd gathers around a large rock where someone is shuffling and flipping cards frenetically, a cigarette dangling from his lips. Money bleeds from one hand to another.

"That's Van, hustling the crowd," the Ringmaster remarks, still staring at the freak show corridor. "He's our Trickster. He meets people at the entrance and gives them a chance to win a dollar."

"A quarter," I correct.

"Hmm?" The Ringmaster frowns and looks over at the gambling mass. "Well, it's supposed to be a dollar. He must be pocketing the difference. I'll have to talk to him about that."

He nods for me to follow and we circle the big top. I can hear the rushing sound of a highway somewhere nearby but can't see it. Tops of buildings jut above the trees that outline the clearing.

The Ringmaster levels a long finger at one of the trees. A figure is doing one-handed pull-ups on a thick branch.

"That's our Strong Man, Kane. I'm not sure if that's his real name or not. He keeps to himself." I stare as Kane pulls himself up, lowers his hulking frame, then up again, over and over.

We continue around the clearing. The Ringmaster grows quiet. Dancers rehearse with no music near the freak show corridor. Behind the big top, animals are led into an enormous tent by a sinewy old man.

"That's where the animals stay during the run," the Ringmaster says.

"Who's that?"

"Mal, the Animal Trainer."

Mal takes hold of an elephant's collar and begins to lead it slowly into the tent. The elephant halts for a moment and the old man unravels a string of obscenities.

"Have you thought about what you want to do yet?" the Ringmaster asks.

"What?"

"What you want to do. You know, do you want to be an acrobat, or a clown? Do you want to help out behind the scenes?"

A woman now climbs up the center pole of the big top and struggles with the circus's banner: an enormous yellow smiley face on a red background. She attempts to place the flag into its hole, misses, then readjusts her foothold on the pole, and tries again. As I watch her battle the banner and the wind, I feel something land on the back of my left hand.

"Actually, I think I'll just watch the show and hang out," I answer, looking down as a mosquito pierces my skin.

I bring my hand down, smashing it, and its crushed carcass falls to the ground. The mosquito's blood and my own are splashed across my palm.

"Hey! Ringmaster!" someone bellows from across the clearing. Looking up, I see a short fat man in his forties bearing down on us. His pockmarked face is red with anger. He holds a plastic water bottle, which spills onto his shirt as he storms closer.

"Charlie," the Ringmaster explains quickly, "The Circus Manager."

"Ringmaster!" the man yells again, although he's close enough now to whisper and we'd still hear him. He wears a grey jumpsuit with the hood pulled back, and thin hair clings tenaciously to his scalp.

Charlie shoots me an angry look and then stares up into the Ringmaster's face.

"I heard you picked up some kid in Boston but I had to see it to believe it." He sends another threatening glance in my direction. "What do you think this is... a fucking orphanage?" he shouts, spilling more water on himself.

"Relax, Charlie," the Ringmaster says softly.

"Relax?" Charlie screams, his spittle hitting the Ringmaster's face. "I'm trying to run a business here. Don't make me get Mr. Alpe involved!"

The Ringmaster places his hand on Charlie's shoulder and the little man nearly jumps at the contact. The Ringmaster stares into his eyes.

"I know what I'm doing," he says, the shadow of his top hat blanketing Charlie's face.

"The hell you do!" Charlie blurts, avoiding eye contact with the taller man. He bats the hand off his shoulder. "You gotta be crazy bringing some God damn kid into the circus. What about his parents? What about the cops? Have you seen the news today? They're already looking for him! I mean, are you an idiot?"

"It's not like we kidnapped him," the Ringmaster says softly, smiling now. "After all, I remember when you first showed up unannounced... not much older than Daniel..."

Charlie screams something unintelligible into the Ringmaster's grinning face. His water bottle falls to the ground, spilling into the grass. Above their faces, I see the woman at the peak of the big top, struggling to regain control of the banner from the wind. Charlie's hands suddenly shoot out and push me hard onto the ground. He screams obscenities and moves toward me. The Ringmaster holds Charlie back, telling him, angrily, to calm down. I push my nose into the wet grass, ashamed of the tears already streaming down my face.

CIRCLE ONE
THE ACROBAT

CANTO FOUR

I wake from a dream of candles and familiar voices in the rain to the sound of mad cheering. Sitting up, still clothed, I rub crust from my eyes. The window above my cot is dark now except for its moonlit edges. Outside, the circus music plays but the distance makes it sound warbled and sick. I shove my feet into sneakers and walk out into the night.

The trailers resemble hunched animals in the cloud-dirty moonlight. Across the clearing, the big top pulses. The audience claps and coos right on cue. I make my way through the maze of trailers, past the ticket booth, and reach the clearing. In the side-tent, Mal affectionately curses the animals who have already discharged their duties.

Entering the freak show corridor, I pass the Trickster smoking a cigarette.

"Hey," I say quietly.

He grunts and walks out of the corridor. I stare after him for a moment, then turn, pass the Tattooed Man and the Fat Woman and the Snake Charmer, and tap lightly on Harry Carrie's case. She looks up from the book she's reading and smiles.

"How are you?" I mouth.

She nods then peers back into her book.

I turn away, embarrassed, and a little angry too, and find myself looking across the corridor into the yellow eyes of the Geek. Bloody feathers streak his face and neck, and his mouth is shut tight, almost puckered. I smile nervously at him. He doesn't move.

"Thank you," the Ringmaster's voice booms out of the big top. "Good night."

Applause follows and the freaks resume their performance positions. As the Snake Charmer coils a viper around her neck, the tent flap bursts open and the audience pours out. I take a hurried step toward the Geek's case, find myself in the way of a large family, trip trying to get out of the way, am nearly trampled beneath fifty or so grammar school kids with bad haircuts, then give up and stand rigid in the center of the passing throng. The Tattooed Man flexes his painted muscles, the Fat Lady winks at the passing husbands and fathers, but the Geek just continues to stare at me. I push against the bodies to retain my balance. An old woman led by a small girl mumbles angrily at me. Her breath smells like cotton candy and beer.

When the last of them pass, I turn but Hairy Carrie has already slipped out the back of her case. Looking around, I see that the Geek is now crouched in the far corner of his case and pokes playfully at a lifeless chicken. A dirty testicle hangs from his diaper. I move to the flap, swallowing down nausea.

Inside, workers pack equipment away. Mal herds the last of the animals out the back of the big top while the clowns sit in the far ring, talking quietly and wiping their makeup off with damp towels. In the center ring, the Ringmaster stands with the older female Acrobat. She's dusting her calloused hands with baby powder. Sweat runs down the back of her neck.

"...shame they can't make it," she's saying as I approach them. I hesitate but the Ringmaster waves me closer.

"We'll just have to pay them a visit," he says softly and then turns to me. "Delores, this is Daniel."

"Well, well," she says, holding out her powdered palm. "The kid everyone's talking about. Nice to meet you, Dan."

I shake her hand.

"Ready?" Delores inquires, looking up into the Ringmaster's face.

"Would you like to go for a ride?" he asks me.

Hairy Carrie pulls the car up in front of the big top five minutes later. Like last time, the Ringmaster gets into the passenger side while I slide in back next to Delores.

The Ringmaster gives curt directions as we make our way through Providence. While Delores stares at the shimmering lights of the city, I wipe the baby powder onto the underside of the seat.

At length, we pull over and disembark, though Hairy Carrie remains in the car. It's beginning to rain a little and I can smell the pavement.

"Give us two hours," the Ringmaster says into the open window. The Bearded Lady nods and silently pulls away.

Delores leads the way down the walk of a small, well-kept wooden house. The Ringmaster smiles at me as he places his finger against the glowing doorbell. After a few moments, the porch light clicks to life.

The door swings open and a pot-bellied man with a bad toupee and stained wife-beater stands, arms outstretched, laughing raucously. Delores and the Ringmaster start laughing, too, and I look at them for a clue to the joke I've missed. The man pulls Delores into a hug and lifts her, still laughing, then turns, holding her captive, and limps into the house. The Ringmaster smiles down at me.

"Shall we?" he asks.

The living room is lined with paintings of circus scenes. Delores is already seated on a large couch, talking and giggling with another man, while the pot-bellied man stands in the kitchen, pouring drinks. Seeing the Ringmaster, the second man instantly stands up and hugs him warmly.

"This is Daniel," the Ringmaster says as they disengage, and the man punches me good-naturedly on the shoulder.

"Hey, Danny-boy," he says.

"This is Hugh," the Ringmaster says and I smile. Hugh is tall and extremely skinny and has long grey hair pulled back into a ponytail. His eyes shine from behind round-rimmed glasses.

"Hugh," the Ringmaster continues, "is the finest acrobat this country has ever seen."

"The world has ever seen," Delores chimes in from the couch. Hugh rolls his eyes.

"Today, Horace," he calls into the kitchen.

"All right, all right," Horace retorts and limps back in, carrying a tray that holds five drinks. He goes from Delores to Hugh to the Ringmaster and then to me. I reach for one of the sweating glasses.

"I don't think so," the Ringmaster says.

"Aw, come on," Horace answers, winking at me, and holds out the drink.

"I mean it," the Ringmaster says and his voice kills the noise in the room.

"I'll get him a soda," Horace concedes, limping back into the kitchen.

There's an awkward moment of silence and I take the opportunity to sit in a plush red chair facing the couch. Hugh sits back down next to Delores. She places her fingers on his knee.

"It's so nice to see you again," she whispers.

The Ringmaster grins at me and remains standing. Horace reenters, handing me a bubbling glass of soda.

"Thanks," I say.

"No problem, kid," Horace responds, then reaches up and squeezes my nose. A loud honking noise comes from behind his back. He reveals a horn and the four of them laugh. "They used to call me Horace the Handsome Clown," he announces, takes a step, and suddenly falls onto the floor. He starts to get up only to fall again, pretends to hit his head on the table, and rolls across the carpet. They laugh louder. Horace crawls over to the table and finishes his drink in a gulp. They've all finished their drinks, even the Ringmaster.

"I guess I'll just bring the booo-tle in," Horace says and they all continue to laugh. Outside, thunder booms a few seconds after lightning glows against the windows. A tree limb bends close to the glass like a thick, dripping spider web.

"Allez... oops!" Horace shouts as he limps back in and trips dramatically over his own feet. The corked bottle flies at the couch. Hugh feigns outraged surprise and then deftly snatches the bottle out of the air. They roar at this display. Drinks are quickly poured, downed, and poured again. I take a sip of my soda. The rain beats against the roof.

They trade stories about people I don't know but I follow as best I can. The Ringmaster interrupts periodically and provides explanations, but these asides are as confusing as the stories themselves. The explanations come less and less the more everyone drinks. Horace disappears into the kitchen when they finish the first bottle and returns with a new one. He repeats the tripping/bottle-flying routine and they laugh harder than before.

"To the circus," Hugh says after refilling everyone, holding up his glass.

"The circus," they all say, raising their glasses. By the time I've lifted mine, they're already drinking. Horace refills the glasses again. Rain pit-pats against the window.

"Hey, whatever happened to that magician we used to work with? What was his name... Chris?" Horace asks.

"He's still working," the Ringmaster answers. "But I haven't heard from him in a long time."

"I was in the business thirty years and that sumbitch didn't age a day," Horace muses.

"It must be... magic," Hugh says in a deep voice. They smile and finish their drinks. Horace limps into the kitchen and returns with a third bottle. Again, he pretends to trip and purposely loses control of the bottle. Hugh's hand lashes out but his fingers grasp air. The bottle hits Delores's cheek with a loud smack and drops onto the couch. Her cigarette falls to the floor in a shower of sparks.

"Ow, shit," she murmurs, standing and pressing a palm against her face.

"Oh man, Delores, sorry," Horace says, laughing nervously. Hugh picks up the cigarette and places it in the ashtray. They all laugh but it sounds forced. Delores excuses herself and goes to the bathroom. The three men stare at each other but no one says a word until she finally reappears a few minutes later. There's a red blotch on her face. She smiles and kisses Horace and then Hugh on the cheek, whispering something into each of their ears.

Hugh pours drinks. I chew ice.

"You still got that Jacuzzi?" Delores asks, sucking down her drink.

"In a manner of speaking," Hugh answers.

"C'mon," Horace says, rising and limping from the room. The Ringmaster shrugs. We follow Horace through a shadowed hallway into a dark room with a glass ceiling. The rain plays a mad drumbeat above us. Horace hits a switch and floor lights beam up, revealing a large, empty Jacuzzi in the center of the room. The Ringmaster laughs and Horace smiles proudly.

"Ta-da!" he exclaims.

"This is great," Delores says. "God, I have so many memories in this room!" Hugh and Horace exchange a glance and laugh. Delores glares at them in mock anger. "Just turn it on."

"No can do," Horace says, limping around the edge of the Jacuzzi. "All the pipes rusted out and I can't afford to get 'em fixed. It's just a tourist trap these days." Horace suddenly loses his balance, and then jumps into the Jacuzzi with a flourish as if he'd meant to fall. Everyone laughs. Horace sits on one of the Jacuzzi benches and as he does so, I get a glance of his crippled leg... and see that it's not a leg at all... just a shaped piece of wood where a leg once was.

"Why not..." I hear Delores say, and she gets in and sits next to Horace.

Hugh leaves the room and returns with the bottle. He steps into the Jacuzzi and everyone is laughing yet again and waving me in. I step in next to Horace, followed immediately by the Ringmaster on my other side. They refill their drinks. The rain beats mercilessly against the glass roof.

Hugh suddenly stands, says he'll be right back and vanishes out the door, his ponytail swinging against his back. The other three trade quizzical glances but Hugh is back in a moment. He holds a photo album against his chest.

"Oh no, embarrassing pictures!" Delores shrieks.

Hugh sits back down across from me. He opens the album and laughs. He holds it up, revealing several photos of random circus scenes. The other three point, laugh, exchange knowing looks. Hugh turns the page, displays it, then the next and the next, eliciting varied remarks from everyone. They come to one page and stop. Everyone leans in close, attempting to divulge the identity of a fuzzy figure in an acrobat's uniform.

"Who the hell is that?" Delores asks.

"Wait, wait," Horace slurs, rubbing his face with a shaking hand. They're all really drunk now, although the Ringmaster doesn't seem affected. "His name was Homer or something like that. He was with us about a week before he got canned. Remember?"

"Yeah," Delores says wistfully. "Wasn't he the guy who was constantly reading those philosophy books?"

"Right, right!" Horace shouts. "He was trying to get his degree through the mail. What an asshole!"

"What was that one line he kept saying all the time?" Delores asks.

"Uh..." Horace says, shutting his eyes. "Uh, shit, right, uh..."

"God is dead," Hugh says from behind the photo album.

"That's it!" Delores says. "Uplifting guy."

"He was a prick. That's why Teddy fired his ass."

"He was never alive," Hugh announces.

"What?" Delores asks.

"God," Hugh says, lowering the album. "He was never alive in the first place."

Everyone grows silent while the rain taps indifferently above. They finish their drinks and pour new ones. I stare at the bottom of my empty glass and through it can see my distorted sneakers on the porcelain. Hugh continues to show the pictures and they make comments, laughing and drinking.

"Wait. Lemme see that," Horace says, looking drunkenly at the page Hugh holds up. Hugh clumsily hands the album over. A tear falls down Horace's cheek, rolls off his chin, and falls to the Jacuzzi floor. He pushes his face against the open photo album and his low sobbing fills the room.

"Excuse me," he finally says and abruptly stands, nearly losing his balance. He places the album where he'd been sitting. His messy toupee hangs into his wet eyes. He steps out of the Jacuzzi, his wooden leg hitting loudly against the edge, and stumbles out of the room.

"Shit," Delores says.

"What's the matter?" I ask, my voice sounding strange even

to me.

The Ringmaster lifts the photo album and places it in my lap. At the bottom of the page, a younger and thinner Horace smiles. A young boy with clown makeup is perched on his shoulder.

"His name was David," the Ringmaster says. "Horace was training him to be a clown. I think he knew David's parents."

"That's right," Delores confirms.

"During one of our shows in Hartford, there was a big fire," the Ringmaster continues. "A lot of people died. David got caught beneath one of the overturned animal cages. Horace grabbed him but the kid was wedged pretty good under there. Hugh tried to drag Horace outside but he wouldn't budge. Not even when part of the burning tent fell on his leg." Hugh rubs his eyes. Delores stares at the floor. "When the firefighters showed up, they literally had to knock Horace unconscious to get him out of there. David held on for a couple of hours at the hospital but..."

The rain pounds the glass and lightning reflects down against our bodies.

"To Horace," Hugh says, holding up his empty glass.

"To Horace," Delores and the Ringmaster repeat, holding up their empty glasses.

Looking down, I spy one of Horace's tears on the green Jacuzzi floor. Everyone is silent. I wonder when Hairy Carrie will show up. I press my sneaker onto the tear and rub it forcefully against the porcelain.

CIRCLE TWO
THE STRONG MAN

CANTO FIVE

The retarded man shambles over to us.

A set of keys is wrapped around his wrist and he wears a backpack with an upside down trumpet sticking out of it. This is the first time I've seen him since he was shoveling shit under the big top on my birthday. His hair is messy. The Ringmaster smiles at him when he stops in front of us. He wears a dirty t-shirt and jeans that are a little too big. Gnarled toes are displayed between the Velcro straps of his sandals.

"Hello, Micky," the Ringmaster says. "Have you met Daniel?"

"I found a new act," Micky answers, not looking at me.

"Yes?"

"Underwater act. Mr. Atlantis. Straitjacket, chains, the works. He's damn g-g-good," the man stutters, his head shaking. "Been out of work a while but I know someone who knows h-h-him."

"I completely trust your judgment," the Ringmaster says, still smiling. "Can you get him before we leave New York?"

"N-n-no," Micky stammers. He turns and stares at me. "Why are you here?"

"What?" I ask.

"He should know better." He looks at the Ringmaster. "You should know b-b-better."

The Ringmaster closes his eyes and the smile disappears. After a long moment, he opens his eyes and levels a cold stare into the retarded man's face.

Micky takes a nervous step back and then looks me in the eye.

"Just be c-c-careful," he whispers, head trembling, then turns and walks awkwardly away. The bottom of the trumpet glares violently in the sunlight.

"What's his problem?" I ask the Ringmaster.

"Micky just sees things a little differently than most people."

"What do you mean?" I pursue.

"Well, he carries around a set of keys that don't open any-thing. He has a trumpet he can't play. And he doesn't like people he doesn't know."

"So, you keep him around just to pick up shit?"

"No, Daniel," he answers, annoyance creeping into his voice. "Micky is the best talent scout I've ever met. He has contacts all around the country. Don't ask me how. And the acts he hires, unlike the ones Mr. Alpe sends, are always crowd-pleasers. This circus wouldn't still be going if not for Micky. As for the shit, he volunteered to pick up after the animals. I never would have suggested it. He's far too valuable."

On our last night in New York, I'm sitting in the Ringmas-ter's trailer as the noise of the circus booms across the clearing. I haven't spoken to Alicia in days but she's all I can think about.

I step out of the trailer to the beat of distant music. It's a clear night, the horizon slowly melting into a pink haze. I make my way around the trailers, retracing my steps in different directions, humming along with the tunes.

Passing through the same stretch of trailers for what must be the fourth or fifth time, I notice that one of the trailer doors is partially open. It's Kane's, the Strong Man. I look around but everyone is busy with the performance. The audience applauds loudly. Inspired by the cheering, I quickly slip into the trailer.

The smell of sweat assaults me as I search for a light. My foot connects painfully with something and I curse under my breath, the cheering distant now. I find curtains and the remnants of day pour in. Weights and barbells litter the floor where I just smashed my toes. Pornographic magazines are strewn across a coffee table.

Nervous, excited, I look through them but I'm disappointed in myself when the hardcore photos elicit more disgust than enticement.

A filing cabinet stands against the far wall, next to a large unmade mattress. My stomach clenches and I fight an urge to turn and run from the trailer. Instead, I hungrily pull the file doors open.

The top drawer is filled with more pornography, as well as body building brochures and magazines. The second holds weightlifting gloves, support belts, a trophy, and various tickets, coupons, and passes. The bottom drawer contains papers and news articles and photos. I slowly look through them, the music falling away behind me. I peruse what must be dozens of circus photos and then come to a yellowing newspaper article hidden between two paper-clipped photos. I bring the faded print close to my eyes.

LOCAL MAN KILLS WIFE, BROTHER IN SEX SCANDAL
POLICE SEARCH FOR SUSPECT

Beneath the headline, a dark photo of Kane stares out.

I suddenly realize that the music has stopped.

The door crashes open behind me. I turn, falling over, and the newspaper article rips in half in my fingers. Kane is on top of me before I can even open my mouth.

"You little fuck," he hisses.

I hold up the torn newspaper bits as if they'll somehow protect me but he brushes them violently aside and wraps his beefy fingers around my neck. He lifts me off the ground and crushes the air from my throat.

"You little fuck," he repeats.

The Strong Man's face contorts with obscene pleasure as the pressure increases. I claw at his fingers while black dots swirl before my eyes. I can feel drool falling from my outstretched tongue.

Then I hear what sounds like an explosion. Kane suddenly grows an extra arm, then two more, then another, until I realize he's being pulled off of me. There is a lot of banging and slamming and now I'm on the floor. The Ringmaster's blurred face appears above me. He says something and I attempt to smile but fall instead into the blackest sleep I have ever known.

CIRCLE THREE
THE FIRE EATER

CANTO SIX

~~~~~~

Candles *illuminate stained-glass windows. An altar reflects shadows from the rain. I sit in a pew, kneeling, fingers clenched in prayer, listening for familiar voices.*

I wake to the sound of a protracted burp, then rain against metal.

"Smell that burrito, bitches," a male voice shouts. Two others laugh.

I swivel my head, trying to clear my mind of the dream-haze, and realize that I'm lying on a small mattress behind the long seat of a trailer-truck. The road bounces beneath me while the three voices drone on.

"Wait, wait... I got something important to say," one of the voices announces, followed by a deep, guttural fart. They all roar.

"God bless you," says another.

"Damn, your ass stinks, man," the third says.

"That's what your wife told me when she was lickin' it clean," says the first. They all laugh again.

I sit up and peer over the seat. It's dark out and rain pounds against the windshield. They all have beards with bits of food stuck in the hair, and the air up front is thick and smelly. I lay back down more in disgust than from fear that I might get caught eavesdropping.

"My stomach is killing me," the first voice says.

"It's killing me too but you don't hear me complaining," the driver says.

"No, seriously," the first retorts.

"That's what you get for eating all those tacos, you fat fuck," the second says.

"You boys want to mess with me, is that it?" the first yells. "All right, I can play hardball." There is a moment of silence, and then he grunts and releases a volley of farts whose sickening smell even makes it back to me.

"For God's sake, you win," the driver yells.

"We surrender, man," the second echoes.

"Damn straight," the winner mumbles.

A few minutes of quiet ensue while the rain plays over us. I breathe through my mouth.

"Why are we the ones stuck transporting this little punk to DC?" the second asks. "If the cops pull us over and find him, we're the ones who're screwed."

"The Ringmaster had to go ahead and deal with some business shit," the driver says as he leans forward and wipes at the windshield. "Jesus, I can't see a damn thing."

"How much longer till we get there?" the farter asks.

"Don't hold your breath," answers the driver.

"God, I hate DC," the second says.

"It's better than... Hey, what's that?" the driver says. The three grow quiet.

"I think it's a deer," the farter says.

"Speed up!" the second says. "You should see those things explode, especially in the rain."

The cab shakes as the truck gains speed. I sit back up and peek cautiously over the seat. Through the foggy windshield and the lines of rain, I can barely make out a distant grey form.

"Speed up," the second insists, stamping the floor.

"All right, I got it to the metal, you prick," the driver shouts back.

The rain sprays in waves against the windshield. I can't seem to look away although I certainly don't want to see a deer explode. Their beards jiggle with excitement.

The farter suddenly leans forward.

"Shit! That ain't no deer, man, it's a dog. Slow down! Slow the hell down!" he yells.

"What?" the driver shouts back.

"Just stop this piece of shit. We can't hit no damn dog, man. Stop!" the farter commands, glaring menacingly at the driver.

"No way we'll stop in time," the man in the middle says quietly as the driver pushes hard against the brakes.

The truck skids along the road and for a moment I'm sure the driver is about to lose control and flip us down the highway. The other two hold onto the dashboard. I press my mouth against the plastic of the seat. The dog becomes more and more distinct and, just as we're about to hit it, I close my eyes.

The rain pounds the roof.

I open my eyes.

The dog stands defiantly in the headlights, looking up at us, bloody teeth bared. Its fur is soaked. The three truckers stare, mouths slightly open. Beneath the dog, a dead deer is sprawled across the pavement, its stomach and neck ripped to shreds. The driver hits the high-beams and the dog's eyes glow.

"Damn," one of the men says.

As we pull around, I look back in the driver's side mirror. The dog has already shoved its face back into the deer's ruptured stomach, its tail wagging in the darkening rain.

We reach DC just before the sun.

The Fire Eater spits up a long burst of flame.

The small crowd that has gathered for one of his rare practice sessions applauds politely. He licks his lips and smiles.

After a few more bursts, the others begin to drift. I remain, standing before him, my arms dangling awkwardly.

"How are ya, kid," he says, removing something from his mouth. He's got black hair and a thin face and he's pretty tall. He's wearing shorts and a t-shirt. I notice a small burn on the edge of his lips.

"Okay," I answer.

"Can I do something for you?" he asks, squinting at me.

I continue to stare, tapping my fingers nervously against my leg. Behind him, I can see some of DC. The buildings look dirty. The Fire Eater begins to move away.

"Can you...?" I begin.

He stops and looks over his shoulder. The three female clowns pass close by, their high-pitched laughter biting into me.

"Yes?" the Fire Eater asks.

I shuffle my feet, kick at the dirt, then shake my head and quickly look up.

"...teach me?" I finish.

"Meet me in the big top tonight after the show," he says and then slowly walks away.

Mal herds the last of the tigers out the back of the big top, cursing wildly, his thick, veiny hands moving even faster, if possible, than his mouth. The Fire Eater places a glistening green-brown wad between his lips and smiles at me, sweat still apparent on his forehead from the night's performance. The Ringmaster sees us, removes his top hat in salutation, and disappears into the freak show corridor. I look back at the Fire Eater's mouth. He moves the dark clump between his teeth.

"What's that?"

"Oakum," he garbles, grinning. He spits the loose wet mass into his hand. "It's... I don't know... sort of a bunch of tar and hemp and jute fibers twisted up together."

"What fibers?"

"I don't know, they used to put this crap on the hull of ships," he explains.

"Oh, cool."

"Actually, it's pretty disgusting," he laughs, and plops the oakum back into his mouth. He withdraws a small black lighter from his back pocket and lights it.

He starts moving the oakum around in his mouth. The small flame illuminates his face. I notice for the first time that scars crisscross his lips; shadows elongate his face. He suddenly spits a burst of flame just above my head. My eyes go wide as the Fire Eater shuts his lips, the fire disappearing abruptly, and stares down at me.

"Enticing, isn't it?" he asks, a wisp of smoke falling from a nostril. He spits the oakum back into his hand. "I soak this baby all day in gasoline. Otherwise it wouldn't last a whole performance."

"Doesn't it burn your mouth?"

"Well, yeah, at first, but it's like riding a bike, right?" he says.

I stare at him, unsure how to respond.

"Fire's dangerous though," he continues, sitting on the dirt of the center ring. "You gotta be careful. It's got a strange way of controlling people."

"It controls you?"

"No," he says, smiling. "Luckily, no. But I've seen a lot of people burn themselves. Literally and figuratively."

He passes the oakum from hand to hand, palms darkening.

"You ready to give it a try?" he asks.

I look at him again, wordless.

"Whaddaya say, Dan?" he says, proffering the oakum up to me.

I contemplate the dark mass for a long moment. I can make out a face in its contours and smile at the thought.

"Look, do you want to try this or not?" he says loudly, the oakum trembling in his hand, destroying the little face.

"Uh... yeah," I finally answer.

For a moment, I can't lift my hand. I see the annoyance creasing the Fire Eater's forehead so I force my fingers out for the disgusting ball of spit and tar and hemp and fibers from God knows where. The Fire Eater stares, waiting.

Just as I begin to close my hand around the oakum, a voice sounds from behind me.

"Hello?" it inquires, deep but feminine. I use the broken moment of silence to retrieve my unwilling hand. Looking over, I'm surprised to see the imposing figure of the Fat Lady in an unbelievably huge sundress.

It's the first time I've seen her walk. I look away.

"Hello," she repeats, quiet now. The oakum disappears within the Fire Eater's fingers. A smile shoots across his face, and then vanishes when he looks back at me.

"We'll finish tomorrow night," he half-whispers, standing and indicating the front entrance with his eyes. I stand motionless for a moment, confused. "Good bye," he insists.

On my way out, I look at the Fat Lady. She gives me a guilty smile. I disappear into the empty freak show corridor.

Circling the big top, I almost smash into Mal and he curses me as if I'm just another animal. I enter through the rear, quickly scaling the back of the bleachers, settling into the darkness between the top two rows.

The big top is silent.

Peering over the back of the seat, I have to keep myself from yelling out in disgust. In the darkened center ring, the Fire Eater is lying on top of the Fat Lady, his face pushed hard against hers: the flash of a tongue, her eyes partially open.

The kiss goes on for so long that I eventually just sit down in one of the seats. They finally come up for air and the Fat Lady giggles, pushing her sizable nose against the Fire Eater's face.

"Hello to you, too," he says.

The Fat Lady giggles more and wraps her flabby arms around his waist. The flesh covers most of his back.

"Does he know where you are?" the Fire Eater asks.

"Of course not!" she yells, pulling her arms away. Her face contorts into several levels of red. The Fire Eater gets to his knees, which barely fit around her thighs.

"All right, all right," he says, laughing, holding out his stained palms. "I was just curious. Don't have a heart attack." Her face continues to redden with anger but the Fire Eater quickly begins tickling her. They both laugh and soon start kissing again. I look at my feet as the slurping noises reach me.

"Mmmmm..." she moans.

When I raise my eyes, the Fire Eater is sitting up again. His hair is messed. He holds the oakum in his palm, right over her face.

"What's that?" she asks.

He smiles and tosses the oakum in the air. It twirls in the half-light of the big top, a dark brown mass, and then plummets into his mouth. The other hand reveals the lighter.

"Ooooh," she squeals, flesh rippling.

"You like fire?" he asks through the oakum.

"Mmmmm..." she moans.

A small burst of flame shoots over the Fat Lady. She claps and wriggles her hips.

"Does it turn you on?"

"Mmmm... yes."

The Fire Eater spits a larger burst, this time much closer to her face.

"Hey, watch it!" she cries.

"I'm just turning up the heat, baby," he laughs, shooting more fire just over her nose.

"Jesus Christ!" she screams. The Fire Eater wriggles up and pushes his knees into her shoulders. She struggles to get off of her back. The smell of burnt hair reaches me. "Get off!"

Another burst quiets her.

"You said you like fire," he says, caressing her forehead. "I'm just giving you what you want, fat girl."

The Fat Lady writhes in the dirt, eyes glinting.

He leans down again and kisses her for a long moment. Sitting up, he quickly covers her mouth and nose with his fingers.

"You gotta eat if you want to stay plump," he says. The oakum is no longer in his mouth. He holds up the lighter and lights it.

The Fat Lady shakes her head frenetically, tears staining the dirt.

"Eat up," he says, bringing the fire close to her face. She moves her head but the flame follows.

I grip the armrest.

The Fire Eater waits and waits and then suddenly pulls his hand away. A burst of flame shoots forth from between the Fat Lady's enormous cheeks. He pulls himself back to avoid being singed.

"Hot damn!" he exclaims.

The Fat Lady's sobs fill the big top. The oakum dribbles out the side of her mouth. He plucks the sand-coated lump from beside her and stands up.

"Feels good, don't it?" he asks, throwing the oakum into the air and catching it behind his back. He walks toward the shadows but stops short.

"Oh," he says, turning and smiling at her. "Speaking of fire... ten bucks says this circus is gonna burn before the run is over, and I won't be the one who burns it."

And then he's gone.

Loud sobs fill the big top.

When she's done crying, the Fat Lady slowly sits up, looks down at herself, and then begins brushing the dirt off of her large body.

CIRCLE FOUR
THE CLOWN

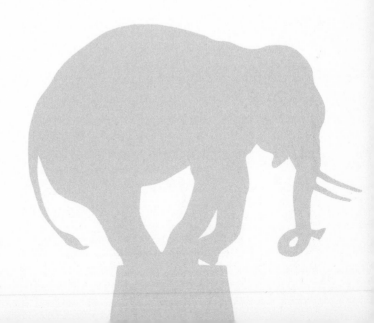

CANTO SEVEN

We're three nights into our Richmond stopover when Pietro, the Lead Clown, agrees to teach me how to juggle. I've heard rumors that he went to medical school decades ago but had washed out when he'd shown up for his final medical exam so drunk that he couldn't even hold a scalpel. We meet in his place the next morning, too early, but he's been up for hours.

His trailer sports trophies, cigar boxes, water color paintings of ten different U.S. cities, pens and pencils in cups of all shapes and sizes; books: fiction, non-fiction, manuals, photo albums, encyclopedias; dozens of porcelain clowns displaying the gamut of human emotion; miniature cars and trucks; hundreds of vinyl albums, but no record player; blackened light bulbs; stacked dishes, all clean; a knife collection; what I think is a dog's skull; several surgical masks pinned to each wall; and dozens and dozens of empty liquor bottles.

"A man goes to a doctor," he says as I survey his trailer. Pietro's skin looks pale and unhealthy without his makeup. "The next day, the doctor calls him," he continues, "And says, 'Well, I've got bad news and I've got worse news.'"

I move a stack of papers and sit down on a metal folding chair. Fighting back a yawn, I focus my eyes on Pietro's mouth, on the joke.

" 'Geez, what's the bad news?' the guy asks. 'You've only gets twenty-four hours to live,' the doctor answers."

I lose control of the yawn and cover it with my palm. The clown stops for a moment, then smiles and repeats, "Twenty-four."

I nod, a little too emphatically.

" 'Oh my God!' the guy yells, 'Twenty-four hours? What the hell is the worse news, Doc?' "

The juggling balls are nowhere in sight. Another yawn begins to creep up my throat and I shift uncomfortably on the metal. As he watches me, Pietro's voice grows irritated.

" 'I forgot to call you yesterday!' the doctor says," he finishes, a little angrily, arms outstretched.

I laugh dutifully.

"What's the matter?" he asks.

"I'm sorry?"

"I thought you said you want to be a clown!" he shouts.

"No, I want to juggle," I explain.

"Oh."

Pietro paces for a few moments, plucks a baseball from behind a pile of folded shirts, and continues back and forth in his cramped trailer.

"Juggling... juggling," he murmurs, throwing his arms up in exasperation. He loses control of the ball and it bangs into an unseen corner. "It's all flash these days. Back in the day... it was the words, the way you crafted a joke. Today, they want knives in the air. Then, slice! There goes an artery, but it sells, it sells!"

"I can come back if—" I start but he shushes me with a twirl of his arm.

"I was always the quickest with a joke, my hat on the ground, the change dropping from the American tourists and soldiers!"

His eyes dart around wildly.

"Ah, I told jokes, but they weren't enough." He turns his watery eyes on me. "You God damn Americans!" he hisses.

"What—?" I begin to get up but he pushes me back into my seat.

I attempt to look out one of Pietro's windows but the clutter conceals the outside world. My legs begin to sweat profusely against the now-warm metal.

"My mother slaved too hard for too little. You hear me?" he shouts into my face.

"Y-yes..." I answer.

"I took to the streets without telling her. I told jokes to the tourists, to the soldiers left over from the war, and I made money, good money, almost as much as she did slaving her fingers to the bone." He displays his fingers but they are hardly thin. I take the pause as an opportunity to adjust my chair closer to the door and inadvertently knock over a pile of clothes stacked on the floor. Nervously, I look up into Pietro's apoplectic face.

"One day I met a soldier, a doctor no less, and the soldier took a liking to me and my jokes. So, I brought the doctor home to meet Momma, under the pretense that she was very sick, but as soon as the two met..." he says, moving excitedly and knocking the pile of clothes into even further disrepair.

Standing up, I catch Pietro's attention and slowly make my way to the door.

"I have to go. I promised the Ringmaster I'd—"

Like a madman, Pietro rushes after me and pins me against the flimsy metal door.

"We had nothing," he whispers, spittle flecking my face. "A table and a few chairs, a bed... but we were a family now."

Slowly, he releases me and steps back. I turn and put my hand on the door handle but his empty voice stops me.

"Momma got pregnant," he says. "But the doctor ran away back to America and left us alone in the basement. As time went by, as her belly got bigger, I noticed how white her face became, how thin her arms... I tried to help but I was no doctor, just a silly little boy. Then, one day..."

"What?"

"One day, I came home from telling jokes to find the police taking her away under a white sheet... My baby sister... not even born yet... she never had a chance... I wasn't there for them... for either of them..."

Neither of us says a word for a painful moment.

Finally, after who knows how long, the Ringmaster's booming voice breaks the silence.

"...I understand that," he's saying loudly.

I take the opportunity to turn and escape from Pietro's trailer. I hear him following close behind. The Ringmaster sees me coming and shakes his head, warning me off. I hide in the shadows of Pietro's trailer. The Clown, however, barrels forward.

The man the Ringmaster is arguing with is tall and blond and, based on the suit he is wearing, very rich. A woman who I assume is his wife stands next to him, staring blankly at a gold watch on her wrist.

"Who the hell is this?" the man asks, glaring darkly at the new arrival.

"This is Pietro, our Lead Clown," the Ringmaster says, "Pietro, this is Peter Alpe, the Owner of the Circus, and his wife, Frances."

"I don't have time for this," Peter says sharply, turning back to the Ringmaster. "Look, attendance is down. If you don't start turning more profit, and I mean now, we may have to close this tour down before it even really gets started."

"Now, Peter..." the Ringmaster says, staring up into the Owner's eyes. "We really should talk—"

"I have to be back in court in half an hour," Frances snaps, grabbing Peter's arm and unlocking him from the Ringmaster's gaze.

Peter reaches into his pocket and removes a breath mint. He unwraps it, pops it into his mouth, and lets the wrapper flutter to the ground.

"Relax, baby, I'm on top of it."

"Don't just throw your shit wherever you want!" Pietro suddenly screams, pointing at the discarded wrapper. Everyone stares at his face as it reddens. "You think because you own this circus you can just litter whenever the hell you feel like?!"

And with that, Pietro lunges forward and grasps Peter's shoulders. The tall Circus Owner grabs Pietro similarly and the two begin tugging at each other. I expect the Ringmaster to intervene but he merely smiles, shakes his head, and takes a few steps back.

Frances, taking one last glance at her watch, steps between the two and attempts to separate them with her thin arms. Neither man seems to notice her. Instead, they increase their struggle and Frances is thrown clear, hard, onto the ground. Her watch pops from her wrist and is trampled beneath Pietro's big feet.

The two men are soon rolling on the ground, throwing punches, until I can no longer tell who is who.

CIRCLE FIVE
THE ESCAPE ARTIST

The rain comes from nowhere and dilutes the fight until it's just two sad old bruised men staring at each other.

Frances looks over at them, her dress a muddy rag, the tears running down her face almost hidden by the rain. The Ringmaster continues to smile. Behind them, a figure appears amidst the shower and slowly approaches. Peter stands and helps his wife up as everyone turns to gawk at the stranger.

He's short but broad, obvious muscles hidden beneath all-black clothing. His hair is black, too, and so are his eyes. He stops in front of us and mirrors the Ringmaster's smile.

"I'm Mr. Atlantis. Micky told me you guys are looking for a new act. So, here I am. Sorry about the rain."

The Ringmaster looks at him skeptically for a second and then turns and points to where I'm hiding in the shadows. "My assistant will show you to an empty trailer on the south wing of the park."

As Mr. Atlantis makes his way over to me, I'm relieved to see that the Circus Owner doesn't even give me a second glance. His angry voice rises above the soft sound of the rain. I nod at Mr. Atlantis and then head off, trudging around the trailers toward the south wing without looking back. As I approach the empty trailer, I realize I haven't heard Mr. Atlantis's footsteps behind me.

"I'm still with you," he says, startling me as I turn around. I laugh, embarrassed, and he's kind enough to laugh in return.

We mount the steps to his trailer, both drenched, when a sound catches our attention. A few trailers away, one of the Lion Tamer's assistants, Chuck, holds a cat face down in a large puddle. He cackles quietly, pulls the terrified animal up, and then plunges its head once more into the muddy water.

Mr. Atlantis walks down, makes his way across the clearing, and grips Chuck by the back of his neck. The surprised assistant loses his grip on the cat and it disappears into the growing shadows of the storm. Without hesitating, Mr. Atlantis thrusts Chuck's face deep into the same puddle. He looks over at me, his face displaying no emotion, and then finally glances back down, pulling the man up and out of the water.

"How's it feel?"

In response, Chuck swivels his head and spits a mouthful of dirty water into Mr. Atlantis' face. I take several steps down, anticipating some kind of violent retribution, but instead, the circus's newest performer smiles and rolls Chuck onto his back, pinning the helpless man against the wet earth.

"You wanna swap spit with me, is that it?"

Chuck's eyes contort in fear as Mr. Atlantis grips his face and squeezes, causing the man's mud-streaked mouth to form a circle. His eyebrows beetle nervously. A line of saliva slowly falls from Mr. Atlantis' lips, hovering agonizingly above Chuck's face, and then drops between his lips. I look away.

A splashing sound finally convinces me to look back up and I nearly yell out when I see Mr. Atlantis standing right next to me, his smile gone. Behind him, Chuck beats a loud and hasty retreat toward the other trailers, occasionally glancing sullenly back, his hatred burning through the rain. Eventually, when he's far enough away that it wouldn't be possible for the Escape Artist to catch him, Chuck opens his mouth and begins swearing at us, delivering promises of vengeance when we least expect it. After a moment or two of this, the smile returns to Mr. Atlantis's face, followed by low, rumbling laughter from somewhere deep in his throat. Although I don't really find any humor in this situation, the combination of the rain, Chuck's nonsensical screaming, and Mr. Atlantis's laughter combine to create a kind of watery song, and I find a smile creeping onto my face in spite of myself.

CANTO EIGHT

Despite the rain that persists during most of our run in Raleigh, the audiences keep growing larger and larger. Mr. Atlantis's performances have proven to be the spectacle that Micky promised: breathtaking escapes from impossibly small water-filled coffins; sleight of hand tricks that make it seem like he can control the course of downward-running liquid; even encouraging audience members to keep him submerged in water tanks until the rest of the spectators clamor for his release, fearful that they might be indirectly responsible for the death of a performer. Each time, Mr. Atlantis emerges with a smile, pushing his black hair away from his eyes. Even Peter Alpe can find no fault with the increased sales, so he has receded into the background, seeming to forget about Pietro altogether, and leaving the Ringmaster to his own devices.

I've taken to showing up at Mr. Atlantis's trailer unannounced. If these surprise visits annoy him, he's never unkind enough to admit it, at least not to my face. Last night, he stunned the crowd by escaping feet-first from a tiny milk jug. There were three standing ovations and the Ringmaster had been forced to make an uncharacteristic mid-show appearance to quiet the crowd and allow the other performers to continue.

I thrust the door open like usual, halfway through my obligatory compliments, but stop dead in my tracks when I realize I'm staring at a beautiful, half-naked girl. Far from surprised by my unannounced arrival, she smiles and walks back to the small bed where Mr. Atlantis sits, looking at me with a bemused look on his face.

"Sorry. I'll come back."

"No, Dan, wait," he responds, stopping me as I turn for the door. "Don't leave. This is Phillipa. She's just visiting."

I take this opportunity to look at the pretty girl in her underwear. She's much closer in age to me than to Mr. Atlantis but I can tell from her eyes that she's seen... and done... a lot. She smiles at me, both of us unsure if we should shake hands, and then she turns and walks into the bathroom, shutting the door quietly behind her.

"Sorry," I say again.

"Stop. Don't worry about it."

Mr. Atlantis gets up off the bed and stretches, his hairy legs arcing out of a pair of black boxers. He throws on a black t-shirt and then steps over to the water cooler he's had shipped in from I don't know where.

"Thirsty?"

I shake my head and watch as he proceeds to drink cup after cup until Phillipa finally returns, now wearing jeans and a *Mr. Atlantis Lives!* sweatshirt that's apparently from a 1995 Las Vegas showcase.

"Have a seat, Dan," Mr. Atlantis says as he crumples the paper cup and tosses it across the trailer into a small garbage can. I comply as Phillipa lies back down, her long brown hair rolling off the edge of the bed. Mr. Atlantis remains standing by the water cooler.

"So you're Dan," she finally says, staring at me with a sly grin. "I've heard a lot about you."

"Really?"

"All good things," Mr. Atlantis quickly counters, seeming to sense my nervousness. I smile but still wonder what he might have said. I've seen myself primarily as a pest, constantly following him around and asking stupid questions about how he does his tricks.

After an awkward moment of silence, he speaks again, seeming to force the words out of his mouth too quickly.

"Phillipa's father is a senator, Dan. Can you believe that?"

Her face immediately darkens as she sits up, pulling her hand away from her head, and points angrily at Mr. Atlantis.

"I told you not to tell anyone that."

"It's okay," he says, holding up his hands. "It's just Dan. He can keep a secret. You can keep a secret. Right, Dan?"

I nod but none of the anger leaves her face. The two of them stare at each other for another excruciating moment and for a second it seems as if they've forgotten my presence altogether. Mr. Atlantis's grin is as infectious as ever but Phillipa isn't smiling back. Finally, as I take a cautious step toward the door, she rises and heads to the bathroom again, slamming the flimsy door as she goes. I swallow nervously and exit the trailer. Mr. Atlantis follows me into the rain.

"Sorry," I mumble a third time, standing on the top step.

"Please, Dan, I'm the one who should apologize. I just... my tongue gets the better of me sometimes."

I watch the rain mat the dark hair against his forehead.

"She's pretty."

"Yeah," he laughs, "Although I don't know what she sees in a geezer like me." I can tell he's lying and he knows it. He watches me fight against a smile of my own. "You ever have a girlfriend, Dan?"

My grin dissipates. Images of Camilla swirl in my brain, and then an unpleasant memory surfaces. Several years ago, my mother made me kiss a neighbor's daughter while both families looked on, my brother howling in the corner, hysterical tears streaming down his face.

"Yeah, a few."

It's his turn to scrutinize my lie but he's too much of a gentleman to call me on it. I walk down the steps and he follows silently through the water.

"I'll walk you to your trailer."

"You don't have to do that. I'm sure she wants to talk to you," I reply, glancing back at his trailer.

"I think she just needs a few minutes to cool off. She'll be fine. Besides, any chance I get to hang out with Dan the Man..."

"Thanks," I say, distracted, unable to get the image of Phillipa's half-naked body out of my head.

The night before our last show in North Carolina, I lay on my cot in the Ringmaster's trailer, staring at the ceiling, listening to the rain pound against the thin metal roof. The show went well tonight, despite the increasing storm from the south, and most of the company has gone into the city for a mini-celebration, including the Ringmaster. Although I haven't seen her since my truncated visit to Mr. Atlantis's trailer, Phillipa's image refuses to leave my mind: the glint of light against her naked shoulder, the smoothness of her legs, her dark hair hanging off the edge of the bed. Mr. Atlantis hasn't mentioned her since that day but she's all I can think about. It takes every ounce of self-control not to ask about her every time I see him.

I sit up in bed, shaking away the melancholy at having been left alone. By now, I'm used to the constant rain so I stand up, put on a pair of sandals, and step out into the storm.

I'm immediately drenched but slosh through the mud, looking up at all of the dark, empty trailers. The only light I can make out is in the freak show corridor; I would visit but I know Hairy Carrie has gone out with everyone else, and I certainly don't want to spend the night locking eyes with the Geek. The rest of the freaks, to be honest, still scare me, too.

As I open my mouth to taste the rain, I suddenly notice a figure out of the corner of my eye. Squinting through the threads of water, I discern the muscle-bound form of Kane, arms akimbo, his gaze seemingly fixed on my small, waterlogged body. For a moment, I'm frozen in terror. He comes closer and closer, his face slowly coming into focus.

"Who's that?" he bellows.

His booming voice frees me from my own fear and I bolt in the opposite direction, away from the Ringmaster's trailer and toward the big top. A slash of lightning bursts overhead, followed almost immediately by deafening thunder. Heart pounding, I sneak into the back of the main tent, scaling the bleachers and settling into the back row of seats, into what I now consider "my spot."

I remain there for what feels like an hour, possibly even dozing, when a noise catches my attention. Across the big top, several yards away from the freak show entrance, a large knife blade slices through the fabric, cutting out a makeshift door. Although completely covered in darkness, I crouch down low and watch as the canvas flap falls forward, revealing a tall man in a rain-drenched business suit. I've never seen this guy before.

The man steps into the big top, wiping the water from his face. He looks around, shaking his head in seeming disgust, and mumbles something I can't hear. Lightning illuminates the canvas roof and the man takes this opportunity to survey the entire tent. I hold my breath as I watch him from between two chairs. Finally, he makes his way to the bleachers across from me and kneels down in the hay, reaching into his pocket and withdrawing a small plastic bag. I watch him fumble with it for a few minutes, the wet plastic slipping out of his fingers, collecting bits of dirt and straw as he tries to extract it from the hay, but he eventually gets it open. He removes a small box and then, from within, takes hold of what look like a small stick, striking it against the box until a small flame erupts, lighting his growing smile. As he holds the flame to the hay, I quickly stand and climb down the back of the bleachers.

Outside, the storm washes over me but I stand still, unsure of where to go, who to tell. My fear of Kane begins to seize me again but I uproot myself and run for the closest familiar trailer: Mr. Atlantis's.

The rain is coming down harder than ever, thunder rumbling violently behind the black clouds, and for a moment it feels as if I'm actually running on the water, weightless and silent.

I trip running up the trailer stairs and fall against the door, causing it to open. Mr. Atlantis peers up from a Houdini biography he's reading and smiles when he sees it's me.

"What's going on, Dan? Midnight run in the rain?"

I open my mouth to reply but nothing escapes except ragged breaths. His face drops as he watches me flounder for words. He stands up, placing his book on a table, and walks over to me.

"What's the matter?"

In response, I grab his arm and pull him out into the storm, pointing across the clearing and finally catching my breath.

"A man... in the big top... starting a fire..."

Just as I say this, headlights illuminate the parking lot on the other side of the clearing. I stare at the growing lights, mesmerized, until Mr. Atlantis grabs me roughly.

"Go to the parking lot. Tell the Ringmaster what you just told me. I'm gonna go to the big top and see what I can do. Send everyone over immediately."

And with that, he's off, padding silently through the puddles and vanishing behind one of the trailers. I hesitate for a moment and then jump from the top of the stairs and sprint for the parking lot.

As I run, I once again have the sensation of gliding across the water, as if I'm riding in a boat. It may be the late hour or the rush of adrenaline or the threat to the circus itself, but I arrive at the parking lot in what seems an instant. The arriving cars are on the other side of the lot and I stop for just a moment to catch my breath. As I stand, hunched, hands on knees, breathing in the rain, I notice a black car close by, its engine idling. This certainly isn't one of the performers' cars, since it's new and obviously very expensive. I walk over and peer into the driver's side window.

Inside, everything is leather and immaculate. I shift my gaze and nearly shout in fear as I realize that someone, eyes glaring, is staring right back at me. It takes a moment for my idealized image of Phillipa to reconcile with the wraith sitting in the back seat. I stand, immobile, for a minute but the distant sound of the Ringmaster's voice pulls me away. With one last glance back at the girl of my dreams, I speed across the water, startling the circus troupe with my sudden arrival.

The Ringmaster looks at me, confused.

"There's... a man... in the big top... fire..." I stutter, pointing across the clearing.

The entire ensemble tenses for a second, all eyes centering on their leader. The Ringmaster nods, as if expecting this.

"Dan, go back to the trailer and wait for me. Everyone else... let's go."

They move as one except for Hairy Carrie, who stares back at me for a moment and then quickly follows the others.

Speeding around the other direction, I can hear them

rumbling toward the big top, so I sprint through the rear entrance and re-mount the back of the bleachers, taking my place within the shadow of the seats.

Mr. Atlantis and the man in the suit stand face-to-face in the center ring, outlined by the growing fire behind them. They speak in terse, clipped tones and I strain to hear them above the pounding rain and crackling hay.

"...ought to kill you for forcing yourself on an innocent girl," the man is saying, the veins standing out on his forehead.

"She lost her innocence long before I got to her, Senator," Mr. Atlantis replies, seemingly unaware of the blaze that'll soon become uncontrollable.

"You scumbag."

Phillipa's father swings his fist wildly but Mr. Atlantis deftly sidesteps the blow. I wait excitedly for him to retaliate. Instead, he stares sadly at the enraged politician, that strange smirk still plastered on his face.

"You picked the wrong man to mess with," the Senator hisses, "and now you and your friends are gonna burn."

Above the red-faced man, the tent sags with the weight of the rain, the bulge glowing defiantly in the blaze's light. The Senator looks ready to throw another fist but Mr. Atlantis's eyes flick over his adversary's shoulder.

"Funny you should mention my friends."

The Senator looks back, an unformed question on his lips, and his face sinks as he takes in the entire cast and crew of his worst nightmare come to life. Snakes slither in the firelight, muscle and fat ripple, and the Ringmaster stands tall in front.

"It doesn't matter!" he screams. "Nothing is gonna stop this circus from burning."

The Ringmaster and Mr. Atlantis make eye contact and then the Escape Artist shifts his gaze to the big top's roof. He screws up his eyes as if confused.

A ripping sound tears through the big top and waves of water splash down, dousing the fire. The Senator is soaked through, his dark suit clinging to his now frail-looking frame, and he looks like a prepubescent boy playing dress up. I almost feel bad for him. Smoke and silence begin to fill the tent, burning my eyes, but I strain to see every detail.

Amidst the dim figures in the center ring, I can make out the Ringmaster's eyes glowing almost preternaturally in the gloom. The performers move forward, seemingly in unison, and the Senator's voice cries out against them, his flat tones barely reaching me. The first scream of pain catches me off guard and I stand up, struggling to see what's happening. But I can't make anything out... other than the sounds of a vicious beating. I climb down the back of the bleachers, my eyes and throat burning.

I'm not sure why I choose to go to the freak show corridor. I guess it's the closest dry spot or maybe I want to get caught. Instead, I find myself staring into the bloodshot eyes of the Geek. As always, blackened feathers fleck his face, and a rare smile emerges as I watch him, his teeth chipped and uneven. His eyes move from me to the entrance of the big top and become fixed there, as if he knows what's going on inside, though the only sound coming from the canvas flap is the liquid puncture of the tent's roof. I pound my fists against the glass, determined to make the Geek look at me again but he won't. I'm soaked to the bone so it takes me a few moments to realize that I'm crying, which makes me angrier, and the more I weep, the harder I slam my hands against the Geek's case.

As the tears and my strength finally fade, I crumple to the ground, exhausted and ashamed and alone.

CIRCLE SIX
THE MAGICIAN

With no explanation, Mr. Atlantis distances himself from me after the incident in Raleigh. I guess it might have been the look I gave him when the performers exited the big top, the Senator strangely absent; or maybe the incident changed something in him that's totally independent of some random sixteen year old kid.

Regardless, I feel increasingly comfortable in the capitol of South Carolina. It's the Fourth of July, and a fieldtrip into the heart of Columbia with the Ringmaster allows me to step out of Mr. Atlantis's shadow. This is the first time since Providence that I've ventured outside of the circus during a run, although the absence of Hairy Carrie stings. But as evening encroaches on daylight, the fireworks that light the sky blast any disappointment out of my mind.

I watch in rapt silence for almost an hour until the conclusion of the fireworks begins, a succession of loud bright blasts, and the audience's shouts hit a crescendo. The Ringmaster says something, loudly, into my ear but I can't quite make it out. When the last of the lights die and the screams and clapping subside, we turn to the distant big top, the smiley-face flag just now taking its place atop the tent.

"What happened the night of the fire? What did you do to that Senator?" I suddenly say, surprised that I even have the balls to ask the question. The Ringmaster doesn't even look at me, just starts heading back to the circus.

We walk the rest of the way in silence.

I know something's wrong as soon as we turn the corner. Pluto, the Lead Midget, is standing in front of Kane, both of them facing us as we approach. A strange crew stands in a semi-circle behind them: Charlie, the Manager, is flanked by the Sword Eater and the Trickster; the Lion Tamer defiantly shakes his hair, Chuck standing nearby, eyes fixed directly on me. Behind this odd collection of performers, a six-foot chain-link fence separates us from the now-assembled circus.

"What's going on, Gerry?" the Ringmaster says through a smile, his top hat tilting.

"We wanna talk."

"About what?"

"Get rid of that kid!" Chuck shouts.

"Shut up!" Pluto yells back, looking over his shoulder for a quick second, and then returns his gaze to the Ringmaster. He doesn't acknowledge me. "We should talk in private."

"You mean without that mob behind you?"

"No, I mean without some kid who could get this circus shut down and all of us arrested."

"The police questioned us weeks ago and have no idea Daniel's here. Besides, I think he deserves to hear whatever it is you have to say about him."

"Fine, whatever," Pluto answers, shaking his head in frustration. "I'm just trying to spare his feelings."

"Fuck his f—" Chuck blurts out.

"Chuck!" several of them yell simultaneously, and he takes a step behind the Lion Tamer.

"Bottom line," Pluto continues, "is that either he leaves, or you both do. Look, it's nothing personal but you know how it works, buddy. We're Carnies. We don't mix well with normals."

The Ringmaster steps forward and stares down into Gerry's

eyes.

"Let us in."

For a moment, I think he'll comply, just like everyone else has when the Ringmaster's voice quiets like this. But Pluto blinks as if sunlight has hit his eyes and he answers "Nah, I don't feel like it."

Up until this point, I've never seen fear or uncertainty on the Ringmaster's face but I see both now. He turns to me and looks like he's going to say something but his face is ashen, and for the first time since I've left home, I feel fear... a huge fear, huge and cavernous... like a church... but in reverse.

CANTO NINE

I'm not quite sure how long we stand there in front of the re-belling performers but the sound of laughter is what brings me back to reality. The three female Clowns stand behind the fence, their makeup half-on, out of costume, lips curled upward in a sickening red. The Ringmaster's eyes are locked on theirs.

"What's the matter?" the Lead Female Clown taunts, running a pink tongue along her teeth. "No one wants to play with you?"

"You're making a mistake, Gerry," the Ringmaster replies, not looking away from the brightly-clad yet strangely attractive Clowns.

"Gerry's making a mistay-ee-ake, Gerry's making a mistay-ee-ake," the Clowns sing and the performers burst into laughter, most of their eyes burning hatred at me. The Ringmaster shifts helplessly.

The female Clowns begin whispering among each other and Pluto takes a step forward.

"So, you need to make a decision. The kid or you."

Kane steps closer too, looking more menacing than ever. A sneer reveals itself on the Ringmaster's face and, as he opens his mouth to respond, I feel a glimmer of hope. However, a shrieking titter from one of the Clowns causes me to look away.

"Hey, Danny, check this out."

A wave of anxiety and excitement washes over me as all three Clowns lift their shirts simultaneously, revealing three very different but enticing pairs of breasts. A smile creeps onto my face despite the situation.

"Daniel, close your eyes," the Ringmaster admonishes.

But I'm paralyzed, mesmerized by the nipples and the supple flesh that surrounds them. The laughter grows louder, almost a hissing now, diabolical, although at this point, I can't tell who's doing what.

The Ringmaster's hand suddenly covers my eyes. I claw at his fingers but he's too strong. Yet the image of the women remains before me, burned into my subconscious like the outline of a distant blaze.

The thunder that suddenly bellows above us is unlike anything I've ever heard before. Wind pushes against my body and the Ringmaster's hand falls away, revealing a scene much changed. The three female Clowns have covered themselves back up, much to my disappointment, and the rebel performers' faces are now filled with fear. Strangely, there are no clouds in the sky but the thunder rolls on unabated. I'm not sure what I see first: the Ringmaster's wry smile finally returning to his face or the strange man in the weathered tuxedo approaching from a side-street, his eyes focused on the motley scene before him.

"What's happening?" I ask.

"This is the Magician we were talking about back in Providence. The one Hugh said always looks the same age."

And sure enough, the Magician's face is cherubic, although his eyes, on closer inspection, seem to reflect years of terrible experience. His skin is dark. He steps between the rebels and us, and fans his left hand in front of his nose.

"You still stink, eh, Gerry?" he says in a voice that is instantly calming and alarming. The Midget looks up to Kane with desperate eyes but the Strong Man seems just as afraid as his tiny counterpart, arms languid at his sides. The three Clowns edge away from the fence, smiles gone. The other performers slowly back away as well.

"This is none of your business, Chris," Pluto says. "You left years ago, so this has nothing to do with you."

"I don't know what you're talking about," the Magician replies. "I just stopped by to see how the Ringmaster is doing." He looks over his shoulder. "How're you doing?"

"Better now," comes the voice above me. I shoot evil glances at Kane and Chuck, knowing I might regret it later.

"They're not coming in here," Pluto insists, crossing his small arms across his chest.

"Chris, if you wouldn't mind, I have a show to host," the Ringmaster says quietly.

In response, the Magician reveals a wand, seeming to pull it from thin air, and waves it several times in front of the rebels. Most of them break into nervous laughter.

"Oooooh," Pluto mocks.

I'm not sure where the first frog comes from but suddenly there they are, one by one, dozens of them, jumping and clinging to the rebels' faces, hands, necks; soundless; and for a minute, I think it's a bad joke. This is our salvation?

But the rebels clearly feel differently, swatting ineffectually at their green- and brown-skinned attackers, no actual damage done, but clearly a creeping fear that pushes them against and then away from each other. The Ringmaster laughs silently.

"When is Gerry going to learn?" the Magician says to no one in particular.

"I suspect," the Ringmaster replies, watching as the frogs disperse, "that someone else put him up to it. I doubt he has it in himself to organize something even this simple."

"Who put him up to it?" I wonder out loud.

The Magician looks at me for the first time and smiles. "How ya doing?" he says, proffering out his hand. "I'm Chris."

I introduce myself and the three of us stand for a moment, quietly, in front of the circus.

"I know you're anxious to get inside," the Magician remarks, "but would you guys like to take a quick walk? I discovered something you might find interesting."

I look up at the Ringmaster, curious but unsure.

"You two go ahead. I need to get prepped for tonight's show."

As my mentor enters the circus, the Magician replaces his wand into nothingness and leads me around the fence, through a tall thicket and down a small, nearly invisible dirt path.

The dilapidated graveyard that sprawls out before us is enormous and I'm surprised that I hadn't noticed it on the drive into the city. But the tall trees completely surrounding it are enough to guarantee that no one on the nearby highway will ever see it. There are only a few granite gravestones. The majority of the markers are simple wooden crosses or glass bottles tied around weathered sticks. Glancing at the few graves that have legible writing, I realize that they stretch back more than a century. The grounds clearly haven't been tended to in a long time. Weeds grow up and over everything. We move among the graves in silence for several minutes.

"What is this place?" I finally venture.

"I think it's an illegal cemetery," the Magician answers, waving his hand and causing small flames to somehow appear midair over the graves.

"What do you mean?"

The Magician smiles at me and then moves on. I quickly follow.

"Not everyone can afford a proper burial or, in some cases, a church won't allow a person to be interred in its cemetery. There are a number of reasons why a family can't or won't bury their loved one in a 'real' graveyard. So, in some communities, people will find a place to bury the 'unworthy.' And I think this is one of those places."

We stop in front of one of the granite tombstones, a small flame flickering just above it. I run my fingers around the fire, searching for string or some kind of magical device, but find nothing

I stare out across the graveyard at the small beacons of light and realize that it has grown even darker during our visit. Neither of us speaks for the rest of our time there but a voice inside me moves from grave to grave, inventing stories for this staggering maze of forgotten souls, every one of them heretics or paupers or both, whether they believed in life after death or not, whether they knew they had the option or not.

CANTO TEN

Halfway through our stay in Columbia, the Magician, Chris, takes me to visit the Fortune Teller, whose name, Cavàl, I hadn't known until now. The Magician calls her "Cal." On the way to her trailer, Chris talks about Cal's "magic" with a slight snicker in his voice.

"...although, she does have quite a knack for the future," he finishes, his voice turning serious.

"The future?" I repeat, her trailer looming.

"But not so good with the present."

I open my mouth to ask another question but the trailer door swings violently open and the Fortune Teller stands before us, wearing a dress at least two sizes too large, an equally sizable smile slipping across her face.

"Chris!" she squeals. "I had a feeling you were gonna stop by today."

"Hey, Cal, you're looking as beautiful as ever."

"Liar," she giggles, ushering us in, her long grey hair sliding across my face, eliciting a disgusted shiver.

"Who's your friend?"

"You know Daniel," the Magician says, picking up one of the hundreds of baubles strewn across the trailer.

"I know where he's been and I know where he's going... but no, I don't know him, Chris."

"Fair enough."

The Fortune Teller shakes my hand and then quickly turns it over, staring at its lines. I glance over at Chris, who simply smiles and whispers an incantation over a crystal ball, causing it to glow slightly. I smile but a deep rumbling sound from Cal's throat draws me back. The rumble finally takes shape as words.

"You are special, the Ringmaster's right."

"What do you see?" the Magician asks, not looking away from the ball, which glows even brighter.

"A church... rain..." she murmurs, wrinkled eyes fluttering. "Candles... flame... a... another boy... pain... a man and a woman... blood-water... animals, wild... fire... No!"

She throws my hand down.

"What?" I ask, following her across the trailer. She slides into the bathroom, the door closing half an inch from my nose. I look over to the Magician but he's still entranced by the crystal ball, which now exudes several colors. I clear my throat several times but the colors increase, brighter, deeper...

"Chris!"

He pulls himself away from the crystal ball as it suddenly goes dark. The Fortune Teller reemerges.

"I have a son a bit older than you," she says, her tone accusatory. She gets closer to me than is comfortable. "His name's Guido."

I force myself away from her, falling into a chair whose stuffing has exploded like premature fireworks.

"Why is he here?" she accuses, pointing a knobby finger in my direction. "Why not my son?"

"Tell me about him," the Magician says, sitting on the floor near the exploded chair. I roll my eyes but he doesn't notice or pretends not to. Cal stands in the bathroom doorway, her plump frame back-lit by phosphorescence.

She stares at him with cocked eyes for a moment and then settles into the broken chair before opening her mouth.

"Don't get me wrong," she starts, her face softening. "Like I said, Daniel's special, but my boy's a writer... a poet. He had a poem published in his high school newspaper when he was your age." I feign admiration but she doesn't even look at me, or at the Magician now. She seems elsewhere, lips silently ticking off some pubescent poem. "He writes to me all the time. The letters are always a little old... God damn mail system! But his words are so... his words are beautiful.

"I'll show you!" she shouts, re-acknowledging us for a tenuous moment, and then she's rummaging through a wobbly wooden stand's small drawer, which is seemingly empty except for a multitude of tarot cards. "In here somewhere. He's got himself a wife now, a gorgeous girl. Haven't met her yet but they're down here in South Carolina, so I'm hoping they'll stop by the circus before we head out, even though they don't know we're here, but they do know that I don't have a car and they have several. Rich bastards! No kids yet but he always liked cars more'n anything, really."

"I have a car," the Magician says quietly, causing her fingers to cease their scavenging.

"I can't find his letters! For the life of me, I need to get organized."

"We can pay your son a visit, if you'd like."

"Oh!" she exclaims, bending over and plucking an envelope off the ground, squealing as she hands it to the Magician. "Here's one of his poems!"

He parts its already-ripped edges and furrows his brow as he feels around inside. He shoots me a quizzical glance as she returns to the wood stand and begins leafing through the tarot cards again. "There are other ones in here. Better ones. I just need to get organized, soon. Now. I just can't seem to... can't seem to..."

The Magician holds the empty envelope in his hand, staring at the return address in the upper left hand corner.

"But that's a good poem, too. Right, Chris?"

"Right," he responds, eyes absorbing the address. "It's a beautiful poem, Cal."

The southern air whips against my face through the open window as the Magician smokes a cigarette, flicking ashes on the floor of his car. He's driving fast, probably too fast since neither of us can wear the broken seatbelts, but the air smells good, so warm, that I want him to go faster.

"So," he says, taking a vicious left-hand curve as I clutch the dashboard, smoke trailing from his nostrils, "What was she talking about? All that stuff about fires and church?"

"Hmm?" I say, barely able to hear him over the wind.

"The church Cal was talking about. With all the candles. "

The wind grows colder and I roll up the window.

"Well, I go to church... I mean, I used to go to church with my family every Sunday. My dad would make us go to six-thirty mass usually, so in the winter it's always pretty dark in there. Except for the candles, really. I like the candles. But not church. I never really liked church."

"Hm."

Houses shoot past us, tiny structures with deteriorating porches, gutted and rusted cars in gravel driveways, and an oc-casional person standing near the road, staring at us as we pass.

The Magician lights another cigarette. I never once see a lighter.

We eventually pull into a large parking lot of a long, flat struc-ture. Windows dot the second (and top) floor, and behind sev-eral of them stand men or women or both, two here, five there, as if they're expecting us.

"What is this?" I ask, watching him get out of the car, unsure if I should follow. "I thought we were going to that guy's house."

"We are. I guess this is where Guido lives."

"Didn't Cal say he's rich?"

The Magician crosses to the front door of this creepy building and enters, never looking back, and I finally find the courage to make my way inside, too.

A frazzled-looking man with a half-day's growth of beard stands behind what I assume is a counter, although in reality it's just an unhinged door on its side, propped up on cinder blocks and sanded down in several key spots. He eyes us warily as we approach; so do several shadows in the doorway that leads upstairs.

"Can I help ya?"

"We're here to see Guido," the Magician says, straightening his bow tie.

"Is he expectin' ya?"

"His mother sent us. She's in town and has something for him."

The man raises his left eyebrow and picks up a grimy telephone receiver from beneath the "counter." He dials and then turns his back to us, mumbling quietly.

"...mother... tuxedo... some kid."

The Magician rolls his eyes at me and I smile. The man finally hangs up the phone, looking at us disdainfully over his shoulder, and mutters, "All right, go ahead up. It's number ten, third door on the left."

On our way up the stairs, the shadows having vanished, I ask the Magician what this place is.

"I think it's some kind of shelter... sort of a hotel for people between... things."

"Kinda like the circus."

We approach number ten and Chris knocks. There's the sound of a terse, hushed conversation and then the door abruptly flies open, revealing a man not all that much older than me, hair hanging in his face, goatee, sweat-stained t-shirt, ripped jeans, barefoot.

He ushers us into a cramped room with blankets covering the windows and clothes strewn across the floor. A young woman sits on the bed, holding a swaddled infant in her arms, staring at a television that displays a blue screen. A porcelain clown stands on top of the TV. The woman tears her gaze away from the screen and looks our way, a wan smile forming on her face. The baby sleeps quietly.

"Aren't you going to introduce us?" the Magician says.

"This is Elizabeth," Guido replies through a frown, sitting on a too-small wooden chair. "And that's our daughter, Jess."

We all nod silent hellos.

"How do you like our satellite TV?" he asks, pointing to the bright blue light and chuckling with no mirth. "It's the only channel you get in this hellhole."

I laugh but Guido abruptly stands up and moves across the room, tearing down one of the makeshift curtains, allowing daylight to invade their sanctuary. The baby stirs, coos, and then falls silent again, her pink eyelids fluttering.

"So, my ma sent ya, huh?" he says, blinking into the sunshine. "How's she doing? Still conning people outta their hard-earned money?"

"Same as anybody," the Magician answers, smiling.

"Psh, no shit," Guido sputters, turning and removing a pack of cigarettes from his pants pocket. He lights one and then proffers the pack out to Chris.

"Thanks," the Magician replies, withdrawing one without seeming to touch it at all.

"You want one, kid?" Guido asks, turning the pack to me. I look over to the Magician, waiting for him to rebuke me for even thinking about it, but he's just smiling down at the baby. Elizabeth smiles too, her face taking on color as attention is paid to her. Slowly, I fumble for a cigarette and place it in my mouth. Guido moves to light it for me but his attention is diverted as the Magician raises his voice, though not his eyes.

"Your mother would like you to visit her. She's in town, with the circus. You should go see her."

The flame hovers close to my cigarette and I both hope and fear that he might actually light it.

"Oh, I should, should I? You hear that, Lizzy? Someone else who wants to tell me what I should do. You two'll get along great."

"Guido, come on, they're guests," she replies, placing the baby down onto the bed and standing up. The flame moves away from me as he lights his own cigarette and turns to her, sneering, silent, his upper lip contorting. Unafraid, she moves to the window and opens it, allowing the smoke to filter out through the filthy screen. The Magician once again lights his own cigarette, though how I'm not sure.

Chris and Guido face each other. I'm sure for a second that fists are going to start flying, and my cigarette trembles and falls from my lips. I want to bend over and retrieve it but I can't look away. They seem to grow closer together but neither of them moves a muscle for what seems a long time. Even Elizabeth turns and stares, concern in her eyes, though for which one I'm not sure. The cigarettes hang at their sides, the disparate lines of smoke curling up and together.

"When I was a kid," Guido finally says, "my mother read my

palm and told me the future. I was… probably *his* age." His eyes flick in my direction and the spell is broken. He steps away from the Magician and leans back against the television. The blue glow emanates from behind, giving him an eerie translucence. Both men stare at each other, taking an occasional drag.

"She told me I was gonna be a writer, a famous writer, and she would make me write these God awful poems that—"

"They're good," Elizabeth interjects. "I read them and they're—"

"—awful poems," Guido insists, shooting her a dirty look. "She would make me write these rhyming poems. God! Even as a twelve year old I knew that rhyming poetry sucks."

"They're good," Elizabeth repeats, a whisper.

"I kept telling her that I didn't want to be a writer. I like cars." He holds up his dirty fingers. "I'm good with my hands, not my brain."

"Stop putting yourself down all the time," she says, louder now, the sunlight spiking out from her hair like a crystalline crown.

"Am I talking to you?"

"Do you ever?" Chris asks, taking a drag on his cigarette.

"Look, man, don't make me—"

"You were telling us about the poems your mother made you write," the Magician counters, blowing the implied threat away in a cloud of smoke.

Silence envelops the room. The baby gurgles and shifts but neither parent looks its way.

"Yeah, so, I kept writing these stupid poems, just to make her happy, even though everyone knew they were awful. And as soon as I turned sixteen, I got into my car and I got the hell away from her. I told her I was going off to college and she believed me. What kind of fortune teller is that?"

The Magician lets out a breath and a pained look sweeps across his face. "She has problems with—"

"—with the present, yeah, so she claims. But if she's so good at seeing the future, wouldn't she have realized when I was a kid that I'm not a God damn poet and that I never will be?"

"There's a difference between what you can do and what you choose to do."

"What are you, a grammar school guidance counselor?" He turns to me. "Is that why you're hanging around with some twelve-year-old?"

"I'm sixteen," I mumble, face reddening.

"Oooh, sorry."

"Don't attack Daniel because you're unhappy with your own choices, Guido."

"Oh, screw you, ya freak. I mean, look at you. You're prancing around in a tuxedo in the shit-bowels of South Carolina, hanging out with some little kid, which is kinda frickin' weird when you think about it, and you have the nerve to question my life? Look in the mirror, pal."

And with that, Guido takes several long steps to the door, opens it, and never looks back. Elizabeth's shoulders are trembling, and at first, I'm sure she's crying. But on closer inspection, I realize it's laughter.

"Are you okay?" the Magician asks.

"I'm fine," she replies, moving away from the window and shutting off the television. "God, I can't stand that blue screen."

"Why are you with him?" I ask.

"Daniel," the Magician warns.

"No, it's all right," she murmurs. "That's a legitimate question, I guess." Her eyes settle on the baby for a moment, glistening as she takes in the image of her slumbering daughter. "You have to understand, Guido's a good man at heart. He doesn't mean to be such a baby. It's just... his mother treated him like one for so long that he doesn't know how to be anything else.

"His poetry really is good. I mean, not great, but that's only because he won't let himself be great. He's embarrassed by it. He's a so-so mechanic but he's got a way with words. Not that you'd be able to tell that from tonight. Sometimes I catch him mumbling lines to himself when he thinks I can't hear him but he refuses to write them down. He's as stubborn as his mother."

"She's in town," the Magician says gently. "She'd like to see you. All three of you, regardless of..." He stares at the baby. "Regardless."

"Don't you think I'd like that, too?" she snaps, and then instantly calms herself. "But Guido would never go for it. He keeps writing to her, each letter a bigger lie. Cars, houses, maids.

Sometimes I wonder if that's the future she saw when he was a kid. The future he created in those letters."

"I'm sure she'd like to see you anyway," I venture.

Elizabeth smiles sadly at me but ignores my comment.

"We're so far in debt, I don't know what to do. Guido gets jobs working on cars now and then, but it's not enough. And now with Jess, it's just gonna get worse. I don't know what—"

"Who's the real father?" the Magician almost whispers.

"What? How dare you!"

"It's a simple question, Elizabeth. No malice intended."

She glances down at her baby for a moment and when she looks back up, I realize that she's just a child too, younger than Guido, and she offers her smooth face up to us without any more anger.

"When I first met Guido, he told me about his mother. I think he still loved her then. When I told him how cool I thought magic was, the fact that he had a mother who could predict the future, he told me he could do it, too. I guess... I wanted to believe that. I let him read my palm and he made up this crazy story about how we were gonna get married and have babies, and he was gonna be a world-famous poet and I would be this insanely successful sculptor."

"You're an artist?" I ask.

"No. But maybe I was once. Or thought I could be, when I was your age. But after Guido told me that, I took a few classes. That was the beginning of the debt. I brought home a couple of the pieces I'd been working on and Guido used them as ashtrays..."

"Which they weren't," the Magician finishes for her.

"No. And to answer your question... it was the instructor. He... he really liked my sculptures... and me. He made... promises. But when I told him about... When I told him, he didn't want anything more to do with me. He even quit the college and I haven't been able to find him."

"Do you love Guido?"

She takes a sudden deep breath, as if the question frightens her. Then she exhales, slowly, and says, "No... no, I don't. But until Jess is older...I guess by then, I might. Maybe..."

She turns away from us, to the window again, and I watch out of the corner of my eye as the Magician reaches inside his jacket.

Glitter falls from his fingers when they finally reappear from the dark confines of his tuxedo. He steps closer to her, so near that I'm sure she'll turn, but Elizabeth doesn't move. Chris holds the handful of glitter up, close to the back of her head, and gently blows until the multi-colored fragments envelop her neck and hair. She closes her eyes, a smile seeping onto her face, and soft giggles bubble up from the back of her throat.

"What... what're you doing?" I ask, confused by her sudden mirth, fearful that he has somehow drugged her.

"Just a little magic," he answers, stepping away from her. "I just gave her a taste of what it could've been like if Guido's prediction had come true."

When we exit the shelter, Guido speaks to us from a shadow beyond the door.

"Tell her to go to Hell."

"What?" the Magician asks without turning around.

"My mother. Tell her to go straight to Hell. I mean, how dare she—"

"Heretic."

"What?" Guido bellows. "What the hell did you just say?"

"You heard me, Guido."

The Magician walks away and doesn't look back. I steal a glance at Guido as I follow Chris back to the car, expecting to see fury but find instead that he's half-turned to the wall, tears glistening in the darkness.

The trip back to the circus takes less than half the time out to the shelter. We hardly speak and don't once meet each other's eyes.

When we arrive outside of Cal's trailer, the door bursts open and she throws up her arms, cackling as if every dream she ever imagined has come true. The disappointment on our faces doesn't seem to register on hers.

"Well? *Well*?" she laughs.

"Just as I suspected," Chris responds, a strained smile emerging. "Four-story house, six bedrooms, a swimming pool, the works."

"I knew it!" she squeals. "And babies? Does my Guido have any babies?"

The Magician inhales, too quickly, but his face retains its false mirth.

"A daughter. Jess."

"Ah, Guido, my Guido!"

She twirls in the doorway as Chris explains that Guido won't be able to attend the circus due to a writer's conference taking place that week in Georgia. When her body slows and she once again faces us, the euphoria on her face is undiminished. For a second, I think she's about to say something more, ask more specific questions about her son and daughter-in-law, but her eyes have the glazed look of the newly-converted and instead she turns away, giggling like the small girl I suspect is hidden somewhere beneath those layers of unwashed clothes and wayward predictions. She enters her trailer, already forgetting that we are there at all.

As we make our way back across the clearing, toward the Ringmaster's trailer, I ask the Magician why Cal isn't able to see Guido's future as a homeless bum; why hadn't she foreseen us visiting him in that hovel of a room?

"Although I don't believe in most fortune tellers, Daniel, Cal has a true gift for the future. But, as with all practitioners of what is often erroneously labeled the 'dark arts,' there is an inverse correlation between their abilities and the realities that surround them."

My blank stare makes him smile.

"Basically, as the future comes closer to Cal and becomes the present, she can no longer see it. She lives with only the fading reminder of what she thinks she foresees. As the future becomes the present becomes the past, she replaces what she has actually seen with what she wishes she saw."

"I feel bad for her," I remark sadly as we make our way around the empty big top.

"Don't," he replies.

CANTO ELEVEN

"**H**ave you thought any more about the reading Cal gave you?" the Magician asks as the freak show corridor disappears from my peripheral vision, and the line of outdoor latrines become visible in the near distance.

"Not really," I answer quickly, Cal's words fresh in my mind, too, and glance up at the sky. "She didn't really say much about my future. I mean, about what I'd, y'know, become."

Stars dot the night sky and I can tell morning, Saturday morning, is not far off, cartoons and sugar cereal a distant memory now, replaced instead with the bright colors of clowns and acrobats, and Chris smiles at me as I stare past him at the twinkling lights in the distant black.

"Well, then, what do you want to be when you grow up?"

I grin at this question, having heard it so many times before, but for the first time, I really think about it, and I'm disappointed when nothing comes to mind.

"I don't know."

"There's nothing wrong with that, Daniel. And there's nothing wrong with changing your mind once you've make a decision either. Believe it or not, I wanted to be a businessman when I was your age."

"Really?"

"Really. And you know what changed my mind? People sort of like Guido and Elizabeth. A nice couple who worked their fingers to the bone but made some bad investments and ended up in debt... so much debt that they could never conceivably claw their way back out."

He smiles. "Being a Magician may not change the world overnight or save lives, but for two hours, for a measly sum that almost any family can afford, I provide an escape from the bills sitting on the kitchen table, while parents laugh with their children, remembering why they have a family in the first place. You see, debt is violence against the truest nature of what makes us human, and through that violence, we affront the very thing in us that is divine."

"You mean, like religion?"

"No, Daniel. Not like religion at all."

Just as I open my mouth to speak again, the sound of someone clearing his throat pulls my eyes away from the Magician. In front of us, several of the rebellious performers have appeared as if from thin air, Kane's massive frame blocking us from the trailers. On either side of us stand the lines of pod-like latrines, and behind us, the rest of the rebels materialize, effectively cutting us off from any avenue of escape. I feel myself take a sharp intake of breath, fear spreading within my chest. Chris merely smiles, staring at Pluto, who once again stands in front, overshadowed by Kane's massive form.

"Geez, Gerry, you still stink," the Magician announces, smiling.

"No more jokes, Chris! I warned you. And no damn frogs are gonna chase us away this time. I said it before and I'll say it again. That kid has to go." He inhales through his nose and then sends a ball of phlegm flying through his tiny lips, landing at the Magician's feet. "Whaddaya say to that?"

"I wasn't joking. You really do smell bad."

And with that, Pluto rushes me, forcing me back against the three female Clowns, who attempt to grab me, while Kane wraps his massive, meaty right hand around the Magician's throat and lifts him well off his feet. Chris doesn't make a sound. Pluto swings his small fists at me while I scramble between the clowns' six legs and manage somehow to break away.

The rebels are momentarily distracted by Kane's booming voice. "Yeah! How you like that, bitch? How does that feel, motherfucker?"

The Magician's face is turning red now, almost purple, but the serenity in his eyes remains.

"Finish it!" the Sword Eater screams, overly excited, withdrawing his blade and slashing it across the Magician's side, drawing blood as well as cheers from his fellow performers.

Kane takes his cue from the growing sense of hysteria and now strangles Chris with both hands. All eyes are locked on the death struggle, except the Magician's, whose gaze crosses over to mine, and the smallest, saddest smile plays across his lips.

As I inhale to scream, a horrible cracking sound emerges from beneath Kane's feet and the wind is sucked from my lungs as the noise grows, amplified a thousand times, a schism appearing in the earth, throwing everyone off their feet. Even Kane loses his grip on the Magician and nearly plunges into the chasm created as the ground shifts, tearing apart like cheap cardboard. Large chunks of dirt and rock erupt from the exposed bowels of the planet and a great shudder rocks us again, causing the latrines to practically explode, tipping over and splashing their contents over a good portion of the rebels, particularly Pluto, who lets loose with a litany of curses that would kill a nun on the spot.

Somehow safe from everything but the stench, I watch in awe as they all forget about one another, attempting vainly to wipe themselves clean while avoiding the gigantic fissures. One by one, they vanish into the shadows; the angry midget's swears still echoing behind him.

When the quakes finally subside and most of the foul ooze makes its way into the smoking crevices, I creep forward, breathing through my mouth. I frantically search the area, holes included, but can find no trace of the Magician. Tears appear on my cheeks and I involuntarily inhale through my nose, tasting their salty flavor as well as the human putrescence that surrounds me.

"Chris!" I yell.

"He's gone," a voice from behind me announces.

I flinch at the Ringmaster's touch and turn on him, savage, blaming him for yet another loss. "What the hell is wrong with this place?"

In response, he takes me by the arm and leads me toward his

trailer.

"Chris came to talk to me earlier... before he took you to see the Fortune Teller," he murmurs, his face shadowed by the top hat. In the distance, the sun is just beginning to crest over blackened mountains, the stars above melting into the emerging light. "He told me what was going to happen tonight. He knew you were going to be attacked."

"How?" I say as the Saturday sun rises before us.

"I don't know," he chuckles. "Honestly, I don't know how he does it. Don't tell Cal, but Chris could do her job anytime, if he wasn't such a damn good Magician." He laughs again, stretching his arms.

As I wipe the final tears from my face, feeling reborn in the shocking sunlight, I realize how very tired the Ringmaster looks.

"What else did he say?" I ask.

He stops and stares at me for a moment.

"He told me to tell you that it's okay. Everything's going to be okay. That there will always be people like Gerry who—"

"Why do you let him stay? Him and Kane killed Chris. They murdered him."

"Really? Did you see Chris actually die? I mean, did you see a corpse?"

"No, but—"

"Listen to me, Daniel. I've seen Chris walk away from situations more dangerous than that. Much more dangerous. And besides, Gerry's not the one we have to worry about."

"What do you mean by that? Who is?"

"I wish I knew," he says, smirking, and then moves on as I trudge after him, my eyes growing heavier with each step.

"Let's go, Daniel. You've had a long day."

I nod and walk behind him, shadowed from the morning light, the fading stars at my back, fissures behind me, the lingering stench fading and then vanishing entirely.

CIRCLE SEVEN

THE BEARDED LADY

CANTO TWELVE

In Athens, Georgia, I attempt to shave by myself for the first time. We just arrived a few hours ago and the Ringmaster is out dealing with the man who owns the lot where we pitched our tents. I had planned on joining him but as I washed my face, I noticed a few intermittent hairs protruding from the skin just beneath my nose. Excited and frightened, I created some half-baked excuse about feeling ill, and waited quietly in the bathroom until I heard the door shut behind him.

I root through his small, weathered dop kit until I find a rusted can of shaving cream. I realize for the first time that I've never seen the Ringmaster shave. As I lather my face, I recall the time my father attempted to teach me how to shave. I must have been six years old, far too young to even really understand what he was talking about. My brother watched us from the bathroom doorway, a strange mix of mockery and jealousy on his face. My father gripped my cheeks too hard and roughly applied the cream, proceeding to do the same on himself. I stared as he took long, slashing strokes along his face, the days-old stubble disappearing into the whitened tap water. After a few minutes, he completed his task, wiped his face with a towel, and then strode out of the bathroom. I stood on the oval green bathmat, shaving cream slowly dripping down my neck, as my brother's face transformed from mockery to outright derision.

"He already forgot about you."

As I draw the Ringmaster's seemingly ancient blade along my throat, my brother's words echo in my mind, and I feel the flesh of my neck rip, a soft gasp finding its way out of the back of my throat. The white foam quickly turns crimson and a veritable river of blood flows down into the sink. I press my hand against the wound while futilely attempting to clean the remaining shaving cream off of my face with my free fingers.

"Hey, Ringmaster! You in there? I gotta question about my act."

The unfamiliar voice reverberates through the trailer, and for a moment I stand frozen, desperately clutching my bloody throat, sink full of hot red water, lines of foam streaked across my pale cheeks. After a few seconds, I manage to take a step toward the door and accidentally kick the small metal garbage can.

"Don't bother hiding. I can hear you in there."

As I open the bathroom door, a figure mirrors me from across the trailer, both of our left hands on doorknobs. The morning sunlight shoots against his back, shielding his identity for a moment, but as soon as I bring the long blond hair into focus, I realize that it's Min, the Lion Tamer.

"You," he growls.

My first instinct is to shut the bathroom door and attempt to barricade myself inside, but there is no lock and my body weight will provide little resistance if he attempts to break it down. For a moment, neither of us moves and the pleasant sounds of morning fill the trailer, juxtaposing the tense stillness within.

"Listen—" I attempt weakly.

"Shut up!" he yells, slowly advancing toward me. I move away from him, allowing the clutter to form a natural maze between us. Our eyes lock. "No one's here for you now, Danny-boy. Not the Ringmaster, or the Magician, or that prick, Mr. Atlantis. First, I'll take care of you and later, when he least expects it, I'll take care of him."

I feverishly cling to my bloody neck as we continue our bizarre dance. He wisely keeps me from the door and I decide the windows are too small for an escape.

"Please…" I whisper, backing against the trailer wall, his outstretched hands moving closer and closer.

The door swings open as Min draws his fist back and the Ringmaster appears, his long face tired-looking and pale.

"What's going on in here?"

The fist goes slack. Before turning around, Min leans a little closer and whispers, "You say anything and I swear to God I will feed you to the lions, you little punk."

With that, he turns and smiles at the Ringmaster. "Hey. I just had a question about my act."

"Daniel?"

They both stare at me and I hold my eyes wide open, afraid the slightest movement will tip either of them off. The Ringmaster's eyebrows beetle and he suddenly steps toward Min, shadowing the man's face with the top hat.

"Min, Min, Min..."

"Wha—What are you...?" the Lion Tamer stammers, resisting, though his eyes glaze faster than anyone else's. The Ringmaster reaches into his jacket pocket and removes a small piece of string. A cruel smile spreads across the Ringmaster's face. The string dances closer and closer to Min's terrified eyes.

Min flails at the string, falling back against the maze of furniture. I shuffle aside to avoid being trampled. The Ringmaster follows him silently around the trailer until Min nearly smashes through the door, throwing it open with a terrified snarl, and disappears into the muted daylight.

As the door clatters shut, I watch as my mentor tidies the mess left in Min's wake. "What was that all about?" he asks without looking at me. "And what happened to your neck?"

"I cut myself shaving," I reply, still holding myself against the wall. "I don't know what Min was doing..." I look down at my bare feet. "Why does everyone here hate me?"

He stops cleaning and glances up at me.

"Not everyone hates you, Daniel."

"Feels like it."

He lets out a breath and removes his hat, placing it on a coffee table. "It's complicated. Some of the performers are jealous... they don't understand why you're here. A lot of Carnies are paranoid... they assume all strangers are bad news. They think everyone wants to burn the circus down or ruin their lives. And I think Min is the worst of them. He just hates... hates for no reason at all."

The Ringmaster frowns, then smiles, picks up his hat, and walks into the bathroom. "Look at this mess," he mutters, but not angrily. I try to pull myself from the wall but several minutes pass before I succeed.

My obsession with following the Lion Tamer around the circus grounds surfaces soon thereafter.

One night, while we're still in Athens, I watch as Min and his two assistants, Chuck and Ness, practice their act in the big top. The lions seem less drugged than usual, more dangerous and feral. I hide in my usual spot in the bleachers as the three men crack their whips and shout staccato commands. As the practice session drags on, Min's patience with his two assistants wears violently thin.

"Come on, Ness!" he yells at one point, his face apoplectically red. "Don't be such a fucking pussy. Stick your head in his God damn mouth. He's not going to bite you unless you're afraid."

Ness, looking incredibly frightened, nods and places his face, inch by excruciating inch, between the rows of the lion's razor-sharp teeth. A drop of sweat rolls down Ness's forehead and falls onto the lion's tongue, causing the creature's jaws to involuntarily flex. Ness jumps back, scaring the lion, while Min screams uncontrollably at his sweating assistant. Chuck grudgingly rounds the lions up, throwing an occasional curse at both men. Soon, Min is berating the two assistants equally and finally storms away, demanding that Mal take care of the animals until tonight's show.

After everyone has cleared out, I make my way down the stairs and walk onto the dirt of the main ring. Lion shit still litters the ground and its stench is ripe.

I hear the tent flap rustle and look up to see Ness reentering the big top. He stops when he sees me, gives a half-smirk, and then walks to a nearby seat where he left his glasses. He places them onto his nose and then just stares at me for a moment.

"You're lucky it's me and not Min or Chuck that came back in here," he finally announces.

"I'm not afraid of them," I lie.

"Hm."

He considers this for a moment and then abruptly turns to leave. Surprised by both his semi-kindness and his sudden departure, I follow after him into the grey evening.

"Why is he so mean to you?"

Ness jumps as if a lion has snuck up on him and not a scrawny sixteen-year-old. He laughs at himself before answering my question.

"I don't know. I guess it's just the way he is. I don't take it personally, especially since he's been the same since he was a kid."

"What?"

Again, the laugh. "Yeah, we grew up together. I forget how new you are. He was my neighbor... we both had shit families, so we hung out a lot. Y'know, tree forts, train dodging, kick the can, all the usual crap."

I nod even though I've never done any of those things.

"When he said we should run away and join the circus, I thought he was kidding." He shakes his head and takes in the small city of tents and trailers surrounding us. "Look at us now." He continues to search the area with his eyes and turns around twice before I ask him what he's doing. "I need to deliver a letter to Carrie, but I don't know where her trailer is. Why is the set-up different in every city? Wouldn't it be easier to pick the same—"

"Who?"

"What?"

"You just said you needed to give a letter to 'Carrie'?"

"Oh, yeah, Hairy Carrie. The bearded lady."

"Her real name is Alicia."

"Really? Huh. Well, Chuck's been on a couple of dates with her and now he wants me to deliver this note for him. God, it's like we're in high school again."

"She's dating him?" I ask, dumbfounded and hurt.

"I know, it's weird. I mean, how can you kiss a chick with a beard?"

I bite my tongue as anger bubbles up from my stomach.

"So, you're friends with her, right?" I nod. "Do you want to help me find her trailer?"

"Okay."

We eventually locate Alicia's trailer and I watch as Ness climbs the steps and knocks on the flimsy door.

"Hold on," Alicia's voice calls from within. I notice that Ness suddenly looks nervous and I wonder if he, too, is harboring affection for my secret crush. Another new friend down the tubes.

Finally, Alicia opens the door and her eyes light up when she sees me standing behind Ness.

"Dan! How are you?"

Before I have a chance to respond, Ness clears his throat and withdraws the letter from his back pocket.

"What's up, Ness?" she asks, her brow wrinkling in confusion.

After stumbling over his own words for a few moments, Ness finally just hands her the letter, and then turns to leave.

"Wait—" I start to say.

"Sorry, but I have to get going. After today's practice run, I don't want Min to—"

"Ness?"

I look up and see tears forming in Alicia's eyes. The note drops from her hand as Ness turns and her fist lands squarely on his nose, sending him sprawling onto the ground next to me. His glasses land nearby, one frame smashed, the other just gone. I look from Ness to Alicia, completely confused.

"Shit..." Ness coughs. "That's the most painful fifty bucks I ever made."

As he slowly makes his way to his feet, Ness spits blood onto the ground and stares daggers at Alicia.

"Ugly bitch," he mutters, then shuffles away, giving me an evil glare as well.

I'm about to chase after him, somehow beat the shit out of him, and then return triumphantly to Alicia's trailer, but when I give one last glance up to her door, I discover that she's already disappeared inside, the discarded letter the only evidence that she'd been out here at all.

CANTO THIRTEEN

For some reason, I enter her trailer without even knocking. It's not something I usually do, especially when it's a woman's trailer, but I want to make sure she's okay.

I find Alicia sitting on a recliner, facing the door as if expecting my entrance. Her eyes are dry.

"Come in, Dan. Shut the door. Do you want some tea?"

Without waiting for an answer, she rises and strides the few feet into the kitchenette and begins preparations for tea. I watch her hands and feel my heart breaking.

"Did I ever tell you that you remind me a little bit of my twin sister, Beatrice?"

"Nuh—" I clear my throat. "No."

A spoon clanks against the cups as she places sugar and then milk and then tea bags into them. The fire burns blue beneath the small kettle.

"It's so strange to be a twin, you know? To have someone out there who looks so much like you. You have a brother, don't you?"

"Yeah, but he's an asshole. We're nothing alike."

"That's too bad," Alicia says, returning to her seat. I sit on the small couch next to her, trying not to stare at her beautiful eyes. Camilla's eyes. "My sister and I get along... got along really well. I miss her."

"I'm... sorry," I stammer.

"Oh," she laughs. "Bea isn't dead. We just haven't talked in a long time. I don't even know where she is."

"I like you," I suddenly blurt.

The teakettle begins to whistle as she stares at me, the slightest blush appearing beneath her beard. She looks like she doesn't know how to respond and I just want to get the hell out of there. Why did I say that?

She rises and goes to the kitchenette, pouring the hot water into our cups. She returns with them, handing me one of the piping mugs. She stares me in the eyes for a long moment, and I feel like I'm about to dissolve like the steam rising from the tea. I want to scream and cry and hold her and run and fight Ness and Chuck and everyone else who hates me, all at the same time. Alicia sits down again and contemplates her tea.

"When I was about your age," she finally says, "I had my first boyfriend. His name was Pierre and he was always so kind to me, so considerate. Although we were... physical, Pierre was usually more interested in talking or cuddling, you know? Not that I minded, of course.

"He was this poet, a wonderful poet, and he used to write me these elaborate poems and they would just make my heart melt. And I blamed myself that I couldn't make him love me the way I wanted him to. But I guess I always knew he was gay... just couldn't accept it. And then I... with my big mouth... this was before the beard, of course... then I stupidly told one of my friends. And she automatically reported back to her boyfriend, who told his friends, and the next thing I knew, Pierre was attacked in the school parking lot and just—" she clenches her jaw and blows into her tea—"and just beaten to a pulp. They found out later that... one of the kids was his own brother. His own God damn brother. It's insane."

She drinks deep. The steam curls up against her moustache and past her eyes.

"Pierre ended up on life support... blind... barely coherent or even alive. I visited him every day but he never acknowledged me... maybe he couldn't. I don't know if his family ever visited. In the end, he somehow found the strength to pull the plug on himself."

"I'm sorry," I reply feebly. "But... you know I'm not gay, right?"

She smiles sadly at me and laughs. "I know. I didn't mean to imply that."

"Was that your only boyfriend?" I ask hopefully.

"No... no, though I wish he had been. A couple years later, just after I finished high school and moved out of my house, I started working at a convenience store part-time. I was also going to community college and my beard was still pretty thin. I was bleaching it, so most people didn't notice. Anyway, the manager of the store kept hitting on me, telling me how gorgeous I looked in that dirty black smock and I guess I just hadn't been complimented in a while, because I fell for it."

"What was his name?"

"Oh... Andy... His name was Andy. Well, actually, I think his real name was Jacob but he went by his middle name. He was... like a wolf. He knew what he wanted and he just took it. Not really all that good looking but just had this charisma, you know? But it got bad fast. I moved in with him and my grades started slipping. Some nights I'd wake up and he'd be... well, he did stuff to me without asking. And whenever I got mad about it, he'd get even more pissed off than me, even though he was the one who was wrong. And he... he started hitting me."

"What?"

"Oh, Dan, it's so hard to explain. You think to yourself, 'I'm better than this. I deserve more than this.' But you still go back. You convince yourself it'll be different this time, that he does love you and just needs to figure out how to say it without hurting you."

"Did he stop?"

That smile again. "No. Of course not. He got worse. As my beard came in thicker, he became more and more violent. I bleached it every morning but he thought it was disgusting. And then he... he burned me one night. With a lighter."

"Jesus!"

"I know. I think it started as a joke at first... well, his kind of joke. He tried to burn the hair on my face and said he was only kidding ... even apologized. But then it kept happening and he stopped saying sorry. And of course, he drank. Drank all of the time. And the more he drank... Well, you know."

"Asshole."

She smiles her beautiful smile. "Exactly."

"You're too good for that kind of jerk."

"I know that now. I just wish I could've figured it out back then. Although... eventually... I did"

"How?"

Alicia takes a deep breath and a strange shudder shakes her face. She looks to the window, lost.

"I never even found out his name. Andy set me up with him. Well, 'set up' is too nice a way of putting it. Andy had this second cousin who... had trouble meeting women. Andy owed him a favor or something, and he told me that I had better do whatever the cousin wanted or the burns would be getting a lot worse. By this point, I was so afraid of him that I would've done almost anything.

"So... Andy went out for the night with a bunch of his friends and, about half an hour later, I heard a car pull up onto the gravel driveway. I started crying but I remember wiping the tears away immediately... I didn't want the cousin thinking I was as pathetic as I felt."

Alicia reaches over and grabs a pack of cigarettes. She lights one, using a lighter hidden in the pack itself, and blows the smoke against the low ceiling. It curls out and vanishes into the growing shadows.

"What happened?" I venture, excited and ashamed by the story. She contemplates me for a moment as if I'm a complete stranger, and then graces me with her rueful smile.

"He knocked on the door and I let him in. He was cute... much better looking than Andy, but he had this sadness that seemed to sap everything out of him. Bags under his eyes, mumbly voice, stooped posture. Something had happened to him, something bad, though I never found out what."

"Did you...?"

"What? Sleep with him?"

Her tone has suddenly grown sharp and I wonder if perhaps I've crossed a line. Outside, the nighttime chatter is increasing, signaling the preparation for that night's show.

"No," Alicia murmurs. "But I would've if he wanted to. We talked... kind of like you and me, Dan. He reminded me a little of my sister, too, only sadder.

"No, I talked and he listened. He listened to all of my

complaints while I cried and cried. He listened and wiped the tears out of my beard. He told me that he understood and that it was time to leave Andy.

"He was only there for about an hour but he was so good to me and I forgot to even ask him for his damn name! He was an angel, maybe the only man I've ever met that I could have actually loved, and I don't even know his name! What kind of person does that make me? I mean, he hated himself, kept telling me that he had it worse, about how much he wanted to kill himself, and I kept asking for more and more of him, until he actually ran out to his car and gave me a gift. A gift from this man who hated himself."

"What kind of gift?"

She inhales deeply and allows the smoke to slowly dribble from her nostrils, then finally rises and makes her way to the kitchen. She plucks a small glass sphere from a shelf above the oven and shakes it gently. Small fake snowflakes dance violently over a serene Christmas scene, which I can barely make out.

"I don't even like it," she laughs, returning the snow-globe to its spot. "I hate the holidays. Always have."

"So, where did you go? Did you find a better boyfriend?"

Another peal of bitter laughter approaches with her as she plops back down across from me.

"No. That was the end of men for me. I moved to another small town and re-enrolled in college. But by this point, school and I didn't like each other too much. I only lasted half a semester. I met a girl, though."

"Oh."

"Yeah. Her name was Lana. She was a junior and she was gorgeous. And rich. I mean filthy rich. Beautiful and wealthy. That's a dangerous combination.

"She knew how to spend her parents' money and, for a little while, I thought I had it made. Lana loved my beard, loved her parents' reaction when they met me and when we kissed in front of them."

"Wow."

"Exactly. Of course, Lana had this evil self-destructive side, so I should've known it wouldn't last. Whenever we fought or if she didn't get her way, she would freak out... trash her apartment or slice her arms with a pair of scissors."

"What? Seriously?"

"She wasn't really trying to kill herself. She just cut deep enough so people would notice and feel bad for her."

"How did it end?"

"Well, her parents eventually just got sick of seeing their daughter making out with a bearded lesbian, so they threatened her allowance. That got her attention pretty quick."

"Right."

"As soon as it threatened her fortune, she betrayed me without a second thought."

I stare at Alicia, not blinking, as the shouts outside echo in and out of the trailer.

"I'm sorry, Dan," she says, taking a sip of her tea. "I don't know why I'm telling you all of this. You don't have to stay if you don't want. I think I'm going to skip tonight's show."

"No," I respond, looking her in the eyes. "I want to stay. Tell me more."

CANTO FOURTEEN

"My sister was a great swimmer. She loved being in the water, all the time, no matter how hot or cold it was. Personally, I hate water. I'm deathly afraid of it. I think I almost drowned when I was a kid. I have a memory of some bully pushing me underwater and holding me down... bursts of light flashing behind my eyes... until my sister showed up and saved me. Although she almost got her ass kicked...

"I guess I always preferred fire. It's strange that Andy chose to burn me because, deep down, I think I liked it. When I was a teenager, I would burn myself sometimes, just to see how much pain I could handle. Have you ever done that?"

"No." An uncomfortable silence fills the room.

"Anyway, my sister was a great writer." She reaches into a drawer and hands me a small self-published book of short stories. "She wrote this when she was, like, twenty years old. Paid for the publishing with money she saved delivering papers in the snow and rain for ten years." She laughs humorlessly, crushing her cigarette with malevolence. "Idiot. What kind of frickin' idiot delivers newspapers for ten years?"

"Maybe she couldn't get another job?"

"That's bullshit! She was... she is smart as hell. She just wanted to have as much time after school to write. Didn't want to 'wear herself out flipping burgers' or whatever her bullshit excuse was. Dumb ass!" she yells, rising and storming into the kitchen. She paces back and forth in the small space, eyes darting madly and unseeingly about the trailer. Her hand lashes out and turns the burner beneath the tea kettle back on.

"And she wasted her time, writing and writing and writing, dropped out of college, and now where is she? Gone! Vanished off the face of the earth."

"Maybe—"

"Maybe nothing! She always told me that God would take care of her, that God would protect those who lived the 'good life.' And so she ran away from me, ashamed of me, ashamed of how I was living my life, ashamed of our parents, and tried to live some pure bullshit life, and now where is she? Where is God now that no one can find her, huh? Nowhere! Fuck God! Fuck Him for everything and fuck Him for nothing!" Alicia hurls her sister's book across the kitchen, smashing it unintentionally against the snow globe, which explodes instantaneously.

"No!"

Whitish sand pours down onto the still-hot oven and fills the air with a repugnant, acrid smell.

"No, no, no!" she yells, rushing to the oven and burning her hand on the kettle. She grabs it by the handle and throws it across the room, away from me, where it shatters a tacky vase. The heated water shoots across the room and dribbles onto the oven where it mixes with the sand and runs in steaming and mucous-like lumps to the floor. Alicia's tantrum ceases as quickly as it started and she slowly crumples, sliding down the kitchen wall, her eyes regaining focus. I want so badly to go to her, to hold her, but I sit still instead, caught between the living room and the kitchen, between love and revulsion.

"I'm sterile," she finally says, staring at the burn marks on her hands. "But it doesn't matter. I guess no one will ever love me back but I just don't care anymore. It's over."

I try to say something but my tongue is like sandpaper. Who is this person? What am I doing here?

As I contemplate these questions, Alicia rises unsteadily and stumbles to the bathroom, leaving the door open. I watch her in the bathroom mirror.

Unaware or simply just not caring that I'm watching, she begins to fill the sink with steaming hot water, placing her already-scalded hands beneath its violent stream. Her face contorts in ecstatic agony. Eventually, just as the sink is in danger of overflowing, she shuts the water off and stares at herself for a very long moment. Finally, she opens the medicine cabinet and withdraws a razor. Without hesitating, she splashes the water onto her face and neck and begins shaving her beard. I watch, dumbstruck, as the clumps of hair fall from her beautiful, mysterious skin. And as she shaves, she speaks, hairy water dripping into the sink.

"I have my grandfather's beard. He was an old man, even when I was little. His wife died very young but he refused to date again, let alone marry anyone else. He used to sit in the middle of his house, this huge house, and watch television. He could barely walk. He'd hobble to the kitchen twice a day to eat some toast, maybe drink some ginger ale, but most of the time he spent smack-dab in the middle of the living room, watching TV until his eyes were bloodshot and baggy. He was a war veteran... he'd suffered a horrible wound in combat, although he refused to talk about it to anyone, even my father, his only son, only child. During the war, he was sliced from balls to chin... with a bayonet is what I was told... and he was shot in the right foot.

"My father and I... we didn't get along. He was an awful, awful person when he wanted to be, and the older he got, the more often that was. I found so much comfort at my grandfather's house. I mean, he never looked at me, even when he spoke a few words here and there... he couldn't look away from the TV, but I would talk to him, tell him about my dreams, and he would nod and wipe his eyes or nose with a dirty handkerchief.

"And surrounding him in the living room were shelves overflowing with books. They all belonged to my grandmother, who was a librarian before she died. The rest of the house was completely covered in plastic... the bed, all of the couches, even some of the doors... everything except his recliner... that same recliner out there that I was just sitting in... the books, and of course that God damn television. And all of the plastic was covered with an amazing amount of dust and it got everywhere. I'd just sneeze and sneeze, and he'd giggle like a little girl and try to give me one of his dirty hankies.

"His left leg was incredibly muscular, probably the only

healthy part of his entire body, and his chest and arms were completely matted with grey hair.

"At least once every time I visited, he would suddenly break into tears while I spoke to him, and then suddenly stop, as if nothing had happened. The last... the last time I saw him... we were talking about where I was going to go after high school... this was just before I met Andy... and he started crying, just like every other time I'd visit. But he kept crying that day, silently, and he still wouldn't look at me.

"I remember those tears on his face and the sun setting outside, its beautiful light streaming in through the plastic-covered windows, and the light and the tears made his face look like it was made out of gold. I kissed him on the forehead and left, and I never saw him again."

"Why not?"

"That same night, a fire started in the kitchen. No one ever found out how, and I guess he was either too slow or too old or both to put it out, and he burned to death. His..." she starts to say as her body is wracked with sobs, the razor still making its way across her neck. "He was found in front of the television."

Alicia cries freely now but refuses to stop shaving. As her throat contracts, the razor slices deeply and her blood pools quickly, dripping into the sink. I remain frozen, hypnotized, her grandfather's recliner filling the void between us.

Alicia makes no move to halt the bleeding. She makes eye contact with me in the mirror for the first time since entering the bathroom.

"When I was a girl, I never understood why he cried." She takes hold of the door with her hair- and blood-splattered hand. "But I do now." And she shuts the door on me, leaving me alone with the darkness and the booming sounds of the circus, both as close and as distant as Alicia herself. I try... and fail... to keep my eyes open.

CANTO FIFTEEN

Unsure of how long I've been asleep, I awake to the sound of Alicia making tea again. I half-sit up on the couch, realizing she covered me with a green blanket that features faded images: dancing clowns, ball-balancing seals, and cannonball daredevils. All smiling, all wrong.

Through the haze of the kettle's steam, I search for Alicia's now-unshaven face. Seeing it for the first time, I nearly laugh in anguished pleasure. Her eyes seem larger than before, impossibly big and blue. They look more like Camilla's than ever. Alicia's cheekbones, mostly hidden before, are so prominent that I curse myself for not really noticing them until now. Her lips, red and moist, are slightly puckered as she readies her drink, mouth just open enough to reveal the tantalizingly white and imperfect teeth within. Her jaw is strong and yet subtle somehow. I suddenly realize that I'm holding my breath.

"I love you."

"Dan? Are you awake? Did you say something?" she murmurs through the steam.

Not waiting for an answer, she pours herself a cup of tea and then a second for me, leaving a low flame on beneath the kettle, and makes her way over, stepping on the sand from the exploded snow-globe, proffering a steaming cup out between us. I take it gratefully as she settles into her grandfather's chair. I don't know what time it is but I can tell it's late based on the big top's apparent silence.

"I'm glad you're up. I want to tell you more about my sister. I've been thinking about what I said earlier and I don't think I was being totally fair."

"You're beautiful," I force out while attempting to take a sip.

"What?"

"Your face..." I cough, "Without the beard... you're beautiful. I mean, not that you weren't before but... I mean..."

"Thank you, Dan. That's very sweet of you."

I drown my embarrassment in another sip.

"I loved my sister's writing," she continues as if never being interrupted. "She was so talented, you know? I was... I probably still am jealous. When we were young, before all the trouble started in our lives, she would write for me, just for me. Poems, stories, whatever. Each one was like a treasure. I kept them all locked away so I wouldn't have to share them with anyone... and I started calling her my 'little treasure.' It sounds so corny now but that's really how I felt back then." She pauses. "Daniel?"

"Yes?" I say, looking her in the eye.

"All of this, your time in the circus, it's bound to come to an end." I start to protest but her hand shoots out, silencing me. "Listen. You're destined for something better than this. I can feel it. You have greatness inside of you. But you have the same problem I did: a past that won't let you go. I think... I think it's up to you to let it go. Then you can pursue your own treasure. Do you know what I'm talking about?"

I stare into her beautiful face for a long moment and want to kiss her so badly that it literally makes me ache. Flashes of memory come back to me... of Charlie knocking me down in my first few hours at the circus... of Micky telling me I don't belong... of the Fire Eater predicting that the circus will burn... of Cal giving me that bizarre fortune... and I realize that Alicia is probably right. I want desperately for the circus to be my home but I'm an outsider, and there's nothing I can do to change that.

"I do. I know what you're talking about, Alicia. And... I love you."

The sadness that fills her eyes at that moment is almost un-bearable. She stands up and takes hold of her mug again, holding its warmth to her still-pink cheeks.

"Oh, Dan," is all she can say for some time. I sip at my tea but for some reason, I don't regret what I just said. "I wish I could say what you want me to say and be who you want me to be. But please," she implores, stepping closer and leaning in, my heart doubling its rate instantaneously, "Please don't be hurt. You're going to find someone, someday, who loves you like you deserve to be loved."

"Why can't it be you? I mean, not now, but someday, when I'm older? When I..." But I don't know what else to say. After another moment, she moves away.

"I'll never find that kind of love, Dan. Trust me, I've tried. No one will ever love me because they'll never be able to accept me as I am. I'm a freak. I'm a curiosity trapped behind a wall of glass. I'm exciting in that way but as soon as the glass is gone, so is the excitement, the mystery. Then I'm just an embarrassment, at best. I'm not a man and I'm not a woman. I've tried loving as both and I've failed as both. I thought finally shaving might help me figure some things out but, honestly, Dan... I've never been more confused in my life."

Despite myself, my eyes begin to grow heavy again.

"No," I protest—against her, against sleep, against everything that keeps her from loving me.

My eyes close again and suddenly she is over me, covering me with the green blanket and gently forcing a pillow under my head. She bends over and kisses me on the forehead, and I feel a tear falling down my cheek even as I'm powerless to stop the slumber that washes against me. She kisses my forehead a second and a third time and I feel the slightest sting of her stubble and I fight back the tears and sleep, and a scream that is trapped somewhere in my throat.

At that moment, the tea pot begins shrieking and she scrambles away to silence it, the sound of her bare feet crunching the errant sand on the floor the last thing I hear as I pull the blanket close and surrender to a darkness that will not be denied.

CANTO SIXTEEN

Darkness. *The sound of running water muffled only slightly by glass and concrete. Then candle after candle after candle simultaneously combust and I slowly come to realize that I'm inside a shadowy church... but not just any church, my church... the one I've always attended. Fog rolls against the candle-lit windows as the rain pounds away.*

A voice behind me shocks me out of my reverie and I turn to face my mother, who wears a nun's habit, but the material is too tight, highlighting parts of her that just shouldn't be highlighted.

I ask her what's been going on since I've been gone and she wraps me in her arms, my face smothered into her breasts, and tells me how worried she's been and how much she misses me. I close my eyes but can still see the scattered glow of candles from behind my eyelids.

She caresses my back with her fingers and I feel like crying with shame. I abandoned my own family... my own mother... and on my birthday...

Then her hands are on my thighs, squeezing gently and I like it, I like it too much, and her voice whispers in my ear and the wrongness of this suddenly washes over me.

I shove her away and she falls to the floor, already laughing, her lips blood red with ridicule, and I've never been more ashamed.

And in that moment, She becomes He, and my father rises up before me and he screams, mirroring my shame and my rage. As the rain's roar increases, I demand to know what's been happening since I've been gone. He bellows at me, repeating over and over again that no one's noticed my absence, not my family, certainly not Camilla, and his anger overflows into his fist and he begins smashing pews and seats with his bare hands. And he's screaming, reminding me how unimportant I am, how he wishes he never got married or had kids, and he raises a piece of a pew, a beautiful ornate piece of wood with intricate carvings, and he hurls it through the closest window, an inhuman growl escaping from the back of his throat. The rain and the fog pour in and I can almost hear laughter beneath the fog as it rolls along the church floor. And my father doesn't stop there. He flails around, knocking candles over, and the church is on fire, so beautiful yet so wrong but I love the colors, I can't help it.

Fire stands like a centurion between me and my father and I open my mouth again to ask what I've missed but he lunges at me through the flames and as he passes through them, unharmed, He becomes He, and my brother stands before me, silently staring with malice from eyes that could just as well be mine.

And now I ask him to tell me what's been going on while I've been gone and he laughs, informing me that he told Camilla that I ran off with another guy. That everyone in the family is glad I'm gone. As he talks, my face grows hotter and hotter, partly from the fire, yes, but mostly, I think, because of the venom dripping from my brother's tongue. Sweat pours down my face as I shake my head, no, and he innocently asks me if I'm feeling hot.

Half-blinded by sweat and tears, I watch helplessly as he sprints away and leaps onto the altar. He turns a semi-circle and faces me, announcing that he'll take care of the fire. Slowly, agonizingly, he reaches into his pants. No.

No.

I surge forward, angrier now than in all the previous moments of his torture and degradation and pain. I'm moving in slow motion, dream motion, but then I'm on him like a hurricane, like the storm that rages against and through the window, and just as unforgiving. I knock him from the altar and punch and punch his face, screaming obscenities only my subconscious seems to know.

I pull the belt from around my waist and quickly wrap it around his neck and I tighten it within my fingers and I pull and I demand to know what's been going on since I ran away. Over and over again I scream the question, and nothing, not even the fading gurgling breath of my dying dream-brother is enough to cool a rage that burns the church and me and my family to ash and smoke.

I awake in steam and confusion. The church's ashes are gone, replaced by a grandfather's weathered chair. Blinking against the steam, I can hear the rain of my dream coming from the bathroom.

"Alicia?"

The bathroom's light seems weaker than I remember it. I stand up, realizing that the shower is on but apparently no one's standing in the stall. Checking the window as I move forward, I see that it's dawn, yet I feel like I've barely slept. The images of the church, the altar, and the fire repeat in my mind.

"Alicia?"

Sand sticks to my sneakers as I make my way across what passes as the living room. It's almost as if I'm walking through fog; I can barely see my hand in front of me.

Inside the bathroom, the steam is at its most dense. It feels like I'm breathing water. As I step forward past the mirror, I bump into something or, more accurately, something bumps into me. I recoil at first but within seconds, I know what it is.

"Alicia!"

I grab her waist and try to raise her up so she isn't hanging anymore but somewhere deep inside me, I know it's too late. I even try to pull the rope from where it's moored in the thin steel girder of the trailer's chasse, but the rope is sturdy with a professional-looking knot.

Even as I'm trying to get her down, I notice with anguish the pallor of her face: a five o'clock shadow just emerging from beneath ice blue flesh.

After realizing that there's no way that I can get her down, I turn and flee that steam bath of terror. Outside, dawn is still just purpling the sky. The steam bursts out with me into the morning's half-light, and I stumble down the steps, collapsing onto my knees, hyperventilating.

Someone clears his throat and I slowly look up, exhausted. What seems like a monster stands before me, flanked by other lesser evils. The steam roils around them and the light at the back of the collective mass shrouds their features in darkness. They seem to wait for me to say something.

"Please... help her."

CANTO SEVENTEEN

"Get up!" the monster demands.

I sit back against the stairs and find myself staring into Pluto's bloodshot eyes. Behind him stand the three female Clowns, inexplicably still wearing their makeup. Pluto leans in close, his breath foul. So close to him for the first time, I realize how young he really is.

"We heard you bawling all the way across the clearing! What the hell is wrong with you? What are you, some fucking baby? Did you wet your bed, you little queer?"

The Clowns squeal behind Pluto. He smiles, satisfied. Trying to catch my breath, I point at the trailer, where the last of the steam is flowing out.

"She…"

"What, she cut herself shaving?"

All four of them erupt in laughter, the Clowns patting Pluto on the back and wiping the tears from their made-up cheeks. I still can't catch my breath and then I realize I don't care.

And before I even know what I'm doing, I tackle Pluto, hold him down, and start punching him in the face over and over again.

Within seconds, of course, I'm on my back as the female clowns pull me off and tiny feet and pink-gloved fists batter at my face and back and groin. After a couple of minutes of this, I squint up through a swollen eye and see Pluto above me again, hurling invectives and an occasional back-handed slap. I find myself smiling at one point, pretending Alicia is still alive and making me tea. The Clowns jump up and down behind Pluto, and I share in their glee.

Soon, others arrive for the tea party and Pluto is replaced by the Ringmaster, who picks me up and seats me once again on Alicia's steps. His top hat's shadow falls across my face.

"Daniel, what the *hell* is going on here?"

Barely able to find my voice, I point at the trailer and weakly bark, "She…"

"What?"

"Dead," is all I can manage.

He curses her under his breath, as if he knew this might happen.

"I'll take care of it," he whispers. "And of Gerry, too."

He pulls away and helps me stand. Others rush past us into the trailer. From within, I can hear anguished cries and arguing.

"Go to bed, Daniel."

"But—"

"*Now.*"

I walk off, refusing to cry. I can feel the bruises taking shape on my face and feel how tender they are to the touch. But I like the pain. It's like I don't even feel it. My mind is a fury, images of Alicia in a burning church filtering through my consciousness.

Something draws me to the freak show corridor. At this time of the morning and considering what's happening across the clearing, it's abandoned. I push through the flimsy plastic doors and approach Alicia's display window. Unwashed fingerprints dot the glass. Tears fill my eyes as I push first my fingers and then my face against her window.

But I don't cry.

Sometime later, I cast off from the window, stumbling back and turning away. I find myself spinning in the middle of the corridor. Faster, my eyes closed, arms flailing, and my mind is free from the images that plague it. I flap my arms like some deranged performer and feel all the blood rushing to my arms, hands, fingers, heated wings tearing away at the stale freak show air. I picture my body spontaneously combusting and consuming the entire circus within minutes.

I blindly smash face-first into one of the glass cases, crumpling like an old doll to the floor. Blood rushes from my nose and reddens the smile I feel emerging beneath it. Looking down at me from the cracked glass are the unbearable yellow eyes of the Geek. He stares at me with bald curiosity, flashing a bizarre smile that mirrors my own. As his twisted grin fades, he points at me for a moment and then at Alicia's empty case, his fingers slowly forming a fist. He suddenly spits at me and I recoil, even as the phlegm splatters harmlessly on the already-stained glass. He cackles like a demon and turns away.

I reach into my pocket and withdraw my wallet, until now unnecessary, remembering how I received it a little more than a year ago, for my fifteenth birthday. I withdraw the few dollars I collected in the weeks leading up to the trip to the circus and then throw the cheap imitation leather wallet into a shadowed corner of the corridor.

Slowly, and with no emotion, I rip apart the bills, one by one, the pieces drifting to the dirt below. Once all of the money has been shredded, I grind the green confetti into the earth with fevered urgency. When nothing remains except a few small green flecks in the upturned dirt, I lie down on top of the buried currency and almost immediately fall asleep.

CIRCLE EIGHT
THE FAT LADY

CANTO EIGHTEEN

O n our sixth day in Mobile, I decide to watch the performance for the first time since my birthday. My face has healed but I still feel numb inside. I've spent the first couple of days in Alabama sulking in the Ringmaster's trailer, cursing Alicia under my breath, bravely refusing food until I'm alone, when I scarf it down like a malnourished dog.

The trailers are uphill from the big top so I make my way haltingly down the sloped clearing a few minutes before the show starts, hoping to avoid the crowd.

The Ringmaster offered to set aside a seat for me in the front row but I declined; instead, I left my jacket at the top of the bleachers hours earlier. I make my way to my coat, surprised to see a beautiful young woman sitting on it. She flashes a closed-mouth smile at me as I sit down next to her, and then the Ringmaster's voice ushers in the darkness.

As the show unfolds before us, I can feel the girl's eyes on me but for some reason, I just don't care. Even the pyrotechnics of the circus, which a few months earlier had dazzled me, seem muted now, as if they were underwater. As the crowd around me applauds and shouts, I feel like a fraud.

During the Lion Tamer's performance, I hear the girl gasp and I chance a look over. Her bright red lips curl back but don't part and her eyes are unnaturally large and attractive. I decide at that moment, with no emotion, to seduce her.

As the Lion Tamer's show roars on, I look at the girl and half-whisper, "This is amazing, isn't it?"

She turns her smile on me and nods, her eyes traveling back and forth between me and the lions. I return the grin and gaze unashamedly at her body. Her breasts are snug beneath a tight yellow t-shirt and the acid-wash jeans look melted on. Her shoes are extremely dirty, so I look back up into her gigantic eyes. She twirls her hair nervously as I stare and she pulls her focus away from Chuck entirely. Her smile slowly fades.

"I work here... for the circus, I mean," I say.

Raised eyebrows greet this information and the smile reappears. She leans in closer to me, listening.

"Would you like me to show you around later? I can introduce you to some of the performers."

She nods vigorously and then looks down, seemingly embarrassed. I let out a breath, pleasantly surprised with myself for getting this far.

"You're really beautiful," I continue, not even caring about her response. "Are you from around here?"

At that moment, another boy approaches us and sits down on the other side of me, uncomfortably close.

"Hey, bud, that's my sister," he practically shouts over the music.

The Lion Tamer's whip cracks again, making me flinch.

For a moment, I feel guilty and Alicia's bloated, shaved face appears like an echo in my mind. I force the image away with disdain. Sitting between the boy and the girl, I find myself the center of both their attention.

"I'm Jason," he says before I have a chance to respond, "and this is Hope. But I guess you already met her, huh?" The Lion Tamer's whip cracks again and this time, it's Jason who flinches. "God," he mutters, "That guy's annoying."

"I'm Dan. I work here, for the circus," I repeat, but if that impresses Jason, he certainly doesn't show it. Instead, he and Hope simultaneously lean in closer to me and I finally realize that something is off with these two. They continue to gaze at me as the show segues into its next phase, the whip cracking one last time and its stark sound falling away instantaneously.

"Me and Hope live less than a mile from here. When we heard

about the Carnies coming to town, we knew we hadda come see 'em. Hope had a feeling we'd meet someone here and when we snuck in and climbed up the back of these bleachers and saw your coat sitting here with no body in it, we knew you'd be just perfect. I got scared for a minute you weren't gonna show up but then here you are."

"Didn't your parents want to come with you?" I ask, desperately trying to make eye contact with any of the circus members, even though I know deep down that the lights are too bright for them to see much farther than the first few rows, let alone the last one. Hope giggles into her hand at my question and Jason clucks his tongue as if I'm a naughty child rather than a kid the same age as him. The Clowns roll onstage.

"Let me tell you something," Jason says seriously. "Our Momma lost her marbles years ago. Don't even know why it happened or how. All I know is that one day she woke up convinced that me and my Pa were dead. We'd stand right in front of her, jump and holler or hit her in the face, but all she'd do is turn to Hope and cry and say how much she missed her husband and son. We thought maybe she was pretending, maybe mad at us for not doing the dishes or taking out the garbage or whatever, but a doctor even came over and just said she had a... psychotic breakdown or something. He offered drugs or to put her away in a hospital but Pa was proud and refused. Plus we didn't have no money, never did, so there's that."

The midgets storm the big top, faux-wrestling with the clowns.

"This went on for a while until we almost got used to it. We'd pass messages to her through Hope, and Momma would do the same, though she didn't know she was doing it, of course. And then... one day she just didn't wake up. No screams of pain or sign that anything was wrong. She just didn't get up out of bed. We buried her in the backyard that night cuz we couldn't afford no funeral."

"You don't have to tell me this, if you don't want," I say, shifting uncomfortably between them.

"I know I don't!" he shouts, his voice masked by a rising strain of music as the acrobats now flip through the air above us. "Just listen! Jesus!

"The next day, our Pa went a little nuts, I guess you could say. He woke up and just started whomping on Hope, beatin' the hell out of her face, blaming her for Momma dying since Hope was the only one she would talk to before she died. I tried to stop him but he just threw me aside and went back to work on Hope." He takes a deep breath and his eyes bulge maniacally. Delores does an impressive triple flip and the audience gasps.

"Why didn't you call the cops?"

"I did! Christ, Dan, will you let a guy tell his story? Jesus!

"The cops came pretty fast after I called and were ready to bust up my Pa something good... they knew him from the local bar... but suddenly Hope blurted out that she just fell down the stairs. I tried to get her to stop lying but she wouldn't, just kept saying over and over again how clumsy she is."

I look over at Jason's sister, still shocked by her beauty, especially after the alleged beating, but she turns away as if ashamed of this part of the story.

"So, the cops left," Jason continues. "Not much they could do if Hope wasn't going to tell the truth. But at least it stopped Pa from hitting her. Me and Hope went down to the river for the rest of the day... I cleaned up her face and we went swimming and stuff... but when we got back, Pa was gone. We waited a day and then another and then kept on waiting but he just never came back. To this day, I don't know where he went or if he's even still alive."

I swallow nervously, wondering what I've gotten myself into. The lights darken as the performers ready themselves for the finale. Frenetic music blares, creating an eerie backdrop to Jason's story.

"I steal to keep us alive, whatever I can get my hands on... even farm animals for food. I don't like killing 'em... that look in their eyes... but the look in Hope's when she's hungry is worse, though she never complains. Hell, she says less and less as time goes along, until now she pretty much doesn't talk at all, and who can blame her?"

They push closer to me again and now I can feel Hope's breasts against my side and I hate myself for how excited this makes me. Jason notices the sweat on my forehead and flashes a smile that makes my skin crawl.

"So, here's what I'm gonna do," he whispers as all the performers fill the three rings, displaying their varied talents, the music kicking into overdrive. "I like you, Dan. Most people pay fifty, but I'm gonna let you have Hope for twenty bucks. A bargain, really. And you can do whatever you want with her... anything." He chuckles. "Well... anything, as long as you don't knock her up."

He takes my baffled silence as intrigue.

"Oh, and trust me, she's good, if you know what I mean," he adds, winking at both of us. I feel Hope giggle soundlessly and I turn to her, lustful and disgusted at the same time. She pushes her palm against her forehead, parting her beautiful hair, and opens her mouth to speak to me for the first time, revealing only a few teeth, and those that do remain are yellow, deadened, sickening.

"Do you want me?" she whispers.

Her putrid breath washes over me and before I know what I'm doing, I topple over Jason, inadvertently hitting him in the face as I escape, and climb down the back of the bleachers, my stomach threatening to revolt at any second. Behind me, the sounds of the finale are warped except for Chuck's whip, which cracks with endless clarity now. I silently beg for the Ringmaster to end the show. The noise and the music fuel my nausea.

I burst from the back of the big top, nearly crashing into a muttering Mal for what must be the hundredth time since I've joined the circus, and sprint toward the line of latrines. I throw open the closest door and I'm assaulted by a combination of stenches: shit, piss, vomit. Reluctantly but unhesitatingly, I place my face just above the wet toilet seat and part with all of the food I had pretended to refuse earlier today.

CANTO NINETEEN

I wait inside that stinking box until the last of the crowd's voices melt away.

Quietly, I step out of the latrine and spit unceremoniously into the already-dewy grass. I feel surprisingly good now and I'm not quite ready to head back to the trailer. I wander around the big top, absentmindedly kicking the detritus of the departed masses, freeing my mind of the disturbing siblings.

At length, I approach one of the practice tents and I can see light coming from inside. Generally, these tents are only used before a performance, so I'm mildly curious to find out who feels the need to hone his or her craft so soon after what seemed to be a very successful performance. Stepping inside, I'm pleasantly surprised to find Mr. Atlantis at rest, submerged upside down in his water tank, wrapped in chains and a straightjacket. His eyes are closed, and his feet, locked in rusty shackles, protrude from just above the water's surface. There's no evidence that he's alive other than a single bubble that lifts from one of his nostrils. Just as I'm about to approach and knock on the glass case, a sound comes from the other side of the tent where another, smaller flap ruffles and reveals Chuck and Ness. I make a move to escape the way I came in but decide against it. Mr. Atlantis is there, after all.

As soon as Ness sees me, the insults spew forth. As much as I want to attack him for what he said to Alicia before she died, there's nothing I can do to him. As Chuck stores equipment for the next day's use, Ness feigns a physical attack on me while mocking my hair, my clothes, even my relationship with both the Ringmaster and Mr. Atlantis.

"Hey, Danny," Ness mocks at the end of his diatribe, "where's your girlfriend, Hairy Carrie? Oh, right. You killed-"

Before he can finish his thought, Chuck grabs Ness by the back of the neck and flings him against the glass tank. The water sloshes quietly but Mr. Atlantis is undisturbed, not even bothering to open his eyes.

"Have some fucking respect," Chuck hisses.

Embarrassed, Ness angrily punches the tank. Again, the water ripples almost soundlessly. Mr. Atlantis doesn't move. Ness pounds against the glass again, harder now.

"Wake up, you freak!" he shouts, punching the glass again and again. Mr. Atlantis doesn't even bat an eye. "Can you believe this guy?" Ness says to Chuck. "Isn't this the douche bag who shoved your face in that puddle?"

Without a word, Chuck smiles and mounts the metal steps that lead to the top of the tank. He stares at Mr. Atlantis's bare feet for a second and then withdraws a pack of cigarettes from a hidden pocket within his gaudy costume. He reveals a book of matches, and without ceremony, lights the cigarette. Before snuffing the flame, though, he holds the lit match to the rest of the book, smiling at me as he does so. The entire book flares up into a mini-inferno and Chuck lowers it quickly onto one of Mr. Atlantis's feet. Ness cackles sycophantically as the smell of burning flesh fills the small tent.

Chuck smokes his cigarette in smug silence, watching as the book slowly burns itself out on Mr. Atlantis's foot. However, both his and Ness's smiles gradually fade as the fire dwindles and then finally disappears without any indication that the Escape Artist is even aware of our presence, let alone in any semblance of pain. In stunned silence, Chuck throws his cigarette into the water and makes his way down the stairs. He shoves his way past Ness and exits through the back of the tent. Ness glares at me with murder in his eyes.

"I'm coming back in a few minutes, you little fag. If you're still here when I get back, I'm gonna bring the Fat Lady in here and drop her on your little friend. I bet he'll notice that."

He departs with a burst of forced laughter and then the tent is as silent as when I first arrived. It's my turn to approach the tank and tap on its glass. Mr. Atlantis's eyes open immediately and a sly smile spreads across his face. In a matter of moments, he frees himself from the straightjacket and chains, reaches up and unlocks the ankle shackles, and pops his head above the water. The deep breath of relief I expect to hear from him never surfaces. He raises himself up onto the platform, muscles rippling, and grabs a white towel. As he dries off, he smiles at me again and asks what's up.

Before I know what I'm doing, I explain all about the siblings and their bizarre story and offer. "I didn't know this stuff was so complicated," I admit tremulously.

Something about this statement piques Mr. Atlantis's interest and he takes a seat, sticking his feet into the water.

"It never makes much sense, Dan. When I was young, I was friends with this kid named Nicholas. Best friends. We did everything together. Hell, we were blood brothers. But there was this girl. This girl we both liked and we both knew that the other liked her but we pretended we didn't. One day, I found out that a bunch of older kids were planning on beatin' the snot out of Nick for something he said to a teacher—ratted one of them out or something like that. I was all ready to tell Nick about it when one of those kids approached me and offered me a ton money... well, it was only twenty dollars but it was a ton of money at the time... anyway, offered me money not to tell Nick what was going on. I don't know what's worse... the fact that I took the money or how fast I did it.

"So, the next day, Nick gets his ass kicked something fierce at the local park. He kept away from them for the first few minutes but once they got their hands on him..."

Silence reasserts itself in the tent and I step away from the tank.

"What'd you do with the money?"

Mr. Atlantis looks at me as if I've struck him and then lets loose with a guttural belly laugh before lapsing into silence again.

"Well," he says at last, "I took that girl out for a date and bought her a present. And it was that night, after Nick got his ass handed to him."

"Did she like the present?" I ask.

"Nope. In fact, she told me it was cheap and cut the date short."

As he stares at his hands, I back farther away until I'm at the tent's entrance.

"Did you ever tell Nick that you knew he was gonna get beat up?"

"Y'know... I never did have the guts to do that," he answers, not looking up.

A few moments later, I leave the tent, neither of us having said another word.

CANTO TWENTY

Although I'm exhausted, I find myself wandering around the clearing in widening circles, occasionally walking slightly uphill and then back down. Eventually, I pass some of the trailers. Due to the strange layout of the venue in Mobile, some trailers are at the top of the hill, some down at the bottom. As my time in the circus continues, I become more aware of disparate social factions and I suspect that the current separation speaks volumes about those divisions. All of the trailers' lights are out except one: the Fortune Teller's.

As I creep closer, I can make out a slight hiccupping sound from within. My sense of the macabre, heightened by Alicia's horrifying demise, brings about images of Cal choking to death on a peach pit, a half-swallowed hard candy, a chicken bone... something. I leap up the trailer's stairs and quickly rap on the flimsy door. The hiccupping suddenly ceases and I strain to hear the sound of a body hitting the floor.

Silence. I knock again, louder, not caring who hears. I refuse to have another death on my conscience. When another endless minute stretches on in silence, I let out a frustrated breath, take hold of the metal door handle with my left hand, and enter.

It's dark inside and it takes my eyes a minute to adjust. The trailer is as cluttered as the last time I saw it and, as I make my way a few steps farther, I struggle not to step on anything breakable.

"Cal?" I half-whisper, afraid I might trip over her corpse at any moment. As soon as her name escapes my lips, the hiccupping resumes behind me, literally causing me to jump, and I whirl around, ready to take on the Fortune Teller's ghost. Instead, I discover her slumped on the floor in the corner, turned away from me, clearly alive and crying like a heartbroken school girl.

"Are you okay?" I ask, stepping closer.

Her head snaps around violently at my question, and if looks could kill, I'd be dead right now. Tears flow freely down her wrinkled face but there's nothing but hatred in her eyes. As she continues to stare and cry, the tears fall from her chin down to her back where they darken the tattered pair of pajamas she wears.

"Are you okay?" I repeat.

"Are you okay?" she counters.

"I..."

"No, you're not okay. You're doomed. Just like this circus. I've seen your future and you die, young and lonely, just the same as you are right now."

"Wait a minute—"

"No! No more waiting!" She raises herself up out of that horrible corner like a wraith and I stumble back, my mouth dry, but she doesn't come any closer. "I knew. I knew what was going to happen to that bearded freak and I let her die anyway. And I'm glad! Do you hear me, you little pervert? I'm glad I let her die!"

"Shut up!" I yell.

She cackles and squats back down, as if she'd never stood. Her head swivels toward me again and the tears continue to drop down her back.

"Yes, yes, I'm a bitch, just like my father always said."

"Your father? What—?"

"He was a shoemaker, you idiot! Don't you see? He was a shoemaker and he always wanted his child, his only child, to take over the business. But how could I explain my gift to him? He called it nonsense and beat my mother when she tried to explain. And you know what's so funny about that?"

I say nothing, fighting an urge to bash this insane woman's face in.

"I wish I was a shoemaker now!" she screams, turning to the wall. I edge closer to the door but something keeps me from leaving. The hiccupping slows and then finally abates. Her voice is barely more than a whisper. "All humans come to a point when they're faced with two snakes that are forever locked in battle. But you have to choose to separate those snakes for their own good. So you step in and you're bitten by them both. Of course you're bitten!"

"What are you talking about?"

"You get bit because those snakes aren't fighting, Daniel, they're fucking! They don't want to be disturbed and in your ar-rogance, you think you're helping but you're just causing more pain and you get yourself killed. That's what pity gets you. It gets you killed. It's a waste of time because the object of pity will turn against you at the first opportunity. Don't you see that? You're as blind as they come but even you must see that!"

The hiccupping resumes again and she raises her hands and presses her palms against the trailer wall, occasionally slapping them gently there, soundlessly, without passion. I turn to leave when I notice a piece of bright white paper on the floor by the door and bend to retrieve it. It's a letter from Guido. Glancing at her briefly, convinced she's already forgotten about me, I scan the words quickly.

I'm not sure if my and the Magician's visit to Guido is to blame, but the letter is a full confession: there is no job, no happy marriage, and no mansion. There is only what we had seen: a hopeless motel room, a blue screen, a conversation be-tween a man and his wife that will never take place. The last line of the letter is simple enough:

"I never want to see you again."

The letter falls from my hand and lands face-down at my feet. I open my mouth to apologize but the words simply aren't there. I slowly back out of the trailer, followed by the uneven hiccups, and close the door with a quiet click.

I become aware of a glow above me and wonder who's turned on one of the big top's exterior lights at this hour. I look up and realize, with a smile, that it's actually the moon: beautiful, bright, and full. It has just passed its pinnacle and is now slowly inching its way toward the horizon.

CANTO TWENTY-ONE

As I look down from the spectacle of sky, I'm startled to see the Ringmaster standing in front of me, top hat in hand. He stares at me with no surprise in his eyes, as if he had expected me to be out and about so late at night.

"Follow me," he says without fire.

And with that, he starts off. I watch his receding back for a moment and then scramble to catch up. He makes his way back toward the big top and then veers left just before entering the freak show corridor. He goes on for a few more paces and then halts just before Mal's large tent. I stop next to the Ringmaster, staring quizzically up at his blank face.

"What're we doing?"

"Wait here," he replies by way of an answer and enters Mal's tent without a further word. Although I can't make anything out within the murky interior, the rank odor of dozens of animals makes its way out to me momentarily and I nearly retch. As I turn away to catch a fresh breath of air, I see the bike rack we've been hauling from location to location for the handful of kids whose parents refuse to drive them to the circus. I hadn't noticed earlier tonight but one bike remains, rusted and sad. Hearing nothing from within Mal's tent, I stroll over to the rack and look the bike over. A weathered black bag is attached to the handlebar by a flimsy strap of Velcro. I look around, absurdly concerned that someone might be looking, and then return my attention to the abandoned bicycle.

My hands lash out with a speed that frightens me and I find myself looking inside the tattered bag. A few wrinkled dollar bills peer back at me. I quickly pocket the crumpled money.

As I step back in front of Mal's tent, the flap opens and the Ringmaster ushers me inside.

The tent is much larger than it appears from the outside; animal cages line every possible space, from the floor to the ceiling. I don't know which is worse: the overpowering stench of feces and urine, or the pitiable looks on the faces of the animals that are still awake. An elephant stares as if it recognizes me and I have to turn away. A lion paces in its too-small cage and then finally circles and lies down with a deep-throated growl. Monkeys jump up and down, against and away from each other, cackling with wild abandon.

Mal is nowhere to be seen.

The Ringmaster motions me deeper into the recesses of this seemingly-unending maze of cages. At length, we reach another flap at the far end of the tent and he pushes through, holding it open for me.

I'm now standing in Mal's small personal side-tent, which is surprisingly well kept and somehow smells nothing like the area from which we just came. Mal stands half in the shadows, scowling at me, but before either of us has a chance to say anything, nine huge dogs materialize from what seems like thin air and charge me, growling viciously, drool dropping from their upturned lips. From within the shadows, Mal grunts and the dogs suddenly stand down, backing away and eyeing me as if unsure whether or not I'll take this opportunity to attack them.

Mal steps from the darkness and looks from me to the Ringmaster, clearly as confused as I am in regards to what we're all doing here. In the warped light of the small tent, he looks like some kind of ancient demon, gruff and imposingly barrel-chested, and I realize with a start that he's holding a gigantic slab of bloody beef over his shoulder. He notices that I'm staring at it and shakes his head as if I'm an especially stupid child.

"It's for the lions, numb nuts."

Nervous, I take a step closer to the Ringmaster and inadvertently kick a huge bowl, causing most of the water within to slosh over the side and onto the ground. I'm not sure who glares at me with more hatred: Mal or the dogs. In the corner, what I assume is a hawk sits on a wooden perch, a leather mask covering most of its face.

"That's my bird, Grizzly. And my puppies, who you've met, are Hellken, Deaddog, Curlybeard, Grafter, Dragontooth, Pigtusk, Catclaw, Cramper, and Crazyred."

At the sound of each of their names, the dogs look up at their master with a fondness that seems almost human.

"These guys are my family," Mal continues. "They're the best family I've ever had. I love them and they love me, and they love each other, too."

As he continues to gush about his animal family, Mal grabs an obscenely large bag of dry food, careful not to drop the slab of meat from off his shoulder, and begins pouring small portions into a series of nine dog bowls, each one emblazoned with its owner's name. The dogs hurry over but wait until Mal is done filling the last of the bowls before digging in.

"It's crazy," he says, looking at us with the closest thing to a smile I've ever seen on the cantankerous old man's face. "They only eat out of their own bowls and they never start without each other. Damndest thing I've ever seen."

He stares at them for almost a full minute without saying anything and I could swear I see tears welling up in his eyes. I almost make a joke about Mal's shocking tender side but the Ringmaster catches my eye and shakes his head.

"Well," Mal suddenly snaps, "I gotta go feed the lions. You guys can wait here if it pleases ya, I shouldn't be more than a few minutes or so." He turns his gaze slowly on me and any tenderness I just saw vanishes immediately. "But watch yourself, boy. Those dogs are gonna still be hungry when they're done, and they don't like you. I can tell."

With that, he disappears into the larger tent, the faintest whiff of shit and piss replacing him and then fading.

"By the way," he says, sticking his head through the flap and startling me, "If you feel like leaving, I wouldn't go through the back if I were you. That's where Micky stores all the animal shit. Once you go back there, you'll be up to your knees and you'll never get out." He laughs at this thought and withdraws his face from our view.

The dogs, finished with their food already, seem to sense that their master is gone for a little while and begin to circle me, seemingly unconcerned with the Ringmaster's presence. I feel sweat trickling down my back and I fight an urge to pee my pants.

"I... think we should leave," I stammer. The Ringmaster doesn't answer but instead looks at me with a bemused expression on his face. The fear nestles deeper in my stomach. "I don't even understand what we're doing here!" I shout, sick of his enigmatic silences.

"Stop whining!" the Ringmaster yells back, a shocking look of anger flashing across his face. "And trust me!"

I look down at the ground in shame and the dogs seem to sense this and they back off, but not far enough for me. Mal re-enters, humming a song I've never heard before.

"Man, they tore through that beef like it was a little kid," he exclaims, clapping me painfully across the back and laughing like a madman. He crosses the small space and withdraws a large chain from a shadowy corner. He runs it through his hands absentmindedly but something about his nonchalance makes me more frightened than ever. "So, Ringmaster," he continues, "I'm guessing this isn't a social call, especially since you brought the brat. Let's get down to it. Whaddaya want?"

Without hesitation, the Ringmaster places the top hat onto his head and says, "I have a favor to ask you, Mal, if you'll hear it."

Mal raises his eyebrows in surprise and then smiles, seemingly pleased with this turn of events, then suddenly shifts his body and lets loose with a guttural fart that makes the dogs, me, and even the hawk jump.

"I guess that means yes!" he shouts.

CANTO TWENTY-TWO

The three of us stand in an odd semi-circle, Mal and I eyeing each other warily. The Ringmaster clears his throat gently and his eyes disappear within the top hat's shadow.

"I realize that you two don't know each other very well but I've thought about this long and hard and I strongly believe that it makes the most sense."

"Get to the point," Mal barks. The Ringmaster looks up and fixes him with a look that clearly unnerves the caretaker. "Sorry."

"As I was saying," the Ringmaster continues, "this may not make sense now but I expect someday that it will. Maybe someday soon." He steps away from us, removing the hawk's mask and pets its head with two fingers. "If anything should ever happen to me, I want to know that I can count on you, Mal, to take care of Daniel."

"What?" Mal and I both blurt, equally incredulous.

"This is bullshit!" Mal rants as I stare at the Ringmaster's back in shock. "If I had known that's what you were gonna ask, I woulda let my dogs tear you to pieces. I ain't no God damn baby-sitter! This is bullshit! Like I don't have enough to do, tending to every God damn animal in the circus, now I have to deal with some pubescent punk who wanted to fuck the hairiest woman I ever seen?"

"Back off!" I yell, stepping closer to Mal, though I know by looking at him that he could take me out without even working up a sweat.

"Enough," the Ringmaster commands, turning around.

"No, it's not enough!" Mal screams, spittle flying from his lips. Even the dogs seem disturbed now and begin to circle us. I swallow nervously, wondering if I'm going to make it out of here in one piece. "You may be my boss but there's only so much you can make me do."

One of the dogs, Grafter I think, approaches the Ringmaster now and, sensing its master's anger, begins to growl. With a glance, my mentor silences the dog and it scurries off into a corner, whimpering.

In fact, all of the dogs are quiet all of a sudden and I think Mal notices this because he's silent now, too.

"Do you remember how we first met, Mal?"

"Oh, Christ, here we go!" the Animal Trainer grumbles, turning around as if he has something else to do but he stops short and stands there with his arms at his sides.

"Do you?"

"Of course!"

"Well, Daniel doesn't know and I think it's a story worth telling. It was, what, twenty-five years ago?" Mal says nothing. "It was Portland, I think... or was it Seattle? Well, that's not important. I had just started my life as a Ringmaster and I'd had a terrible show, just terrible. Botched cues, misunderstandings with the performers, animals out of control, just a mess all around. I got the cold shoulder from the other performers that night, so I decided to head into the city and drown my sorrows.

"I found the perfect little dive bar. The place was pretty empty but I ended up talking to this pissed off guy sitting a couple of stools down." Mal sighs dramatically at this, confirming his entrance into the story. "He was drunk... wasted, in fact, and I guess he felt like talking because I heard it all. He was out on parole after serving several years for embezzlement but he—"

"But he ratted on his friends," Mal shouts, still facing away from us. "So he got off with a light sentence. You fuckin' happy now? Is story time over?"

The Ringmaster smiles at me, pauses a moment, then continues, "We kept talking, for hours it seemed. This guy goes on to tell me that he has to report to his parole officer on a weekly basis and that it's driving him crazy. So I offered him a job with the circus. I don't even think there was an opening at that point, but there was something about that guy that I trusted, something about him that I knew I could depend on. He cheered me up after the worst performance of my life, so I offered him a shot at a new life. And you know what? He took it. And we've been friends ever since."

"I hate that damn story," Mal says, turning around and looking at the Ringmaster as angrily as he can, but I know better.

"So, Mal, do you want to reconsider your answer to my request?"

As Mal mumbles incoherently to himself, I notice Grafter sneaking his way across the room and sniffing around the food bowls. The other dogs, concerned about their master's emotional state, don't seem to notice.

"Well?"

"Fine!" Mal shouts. "Fine, I'll take care of the brat in case someone you piss off feeds you to the lions. Happy?"

"Yes," the Ringmaster answers, smiling at both of us. Mal fixes his eye on his old friend and tries again to look mad, but a reluctant smile surfaces. The Ringmaster holds out his hand and the two men shake, talking quietly among themselves, laughing occasionally. Meanwhile, I watch as Grafter finds an uneaten pile of food in Crazyred's bowl. Grafter looks around as if knowing what he's doing is wrong, but his brothers are circling the two whispering men, their tails wagging happily. Without a moment's hesitation, Grafter wolfs down the food. Suddenly, a deafening screech fills the tent and Grizzly comes swooping down off of its perch, aiming its claws directly at Grafter's unsuspecting eyes.

Grafter turns away just in time but the hawk's talons find purchase across the dog's cheek, spurting blood and spittle across the floor, almost hitting my shoes.

"Grizzly!" Mal screams, pulling himself away from the Ringmaster and entering the fray without a second's hesitation or thought for his own safety. Smelling blood, the dogs move in as well, and Mal and the ten animals morph into a bloody blur, all gnashing teeth, slashing claws, and pounding fists. Mal's curses rise up among the growls and screeches like some kind of inhuman battle cry.

The Ringmaster is next to me before I even see him move. The front entrance is blocked by the deadly battle so we inch toward the back flap, fully aware that the piles of animal feces out there might be just as fatal. We glance at each other, take a deep breath, and exit, ready to confront the mountains of excrement.

CANTO TWENTY-THREE

Only there are no mountains of excrement. No smell. No piles of animal shit. It's a lie. An unfathomable one, but a lie nonetheless. The Ringmaster smirks at me as I stare at a path that leads down a small hill and into a beautiful forest that is otherwise blocked by Mal's large tent. Clearly the old Animal Trainer knew about the path but apparently wanted to keep it to himself for some reason.

"Shall we?" the Ringmaster inquires and starts off down the path. I hurry to catch up and swallow nervously as the trees' shadows engulf us.

We walk for a few minutes, the path partially lit by the bright moon above. The light and shadows along the path hypnotize me, and only the Ringmaster's outstretched hand keeps me from walking off a small cliff at the end of the path. I thank him quietly and then look out over the precipice. Mobile's lights shimmer beautifully below, a silent city on the water's edge. The moon sits perched in the sky above, lighting the buildings and the water and the horizon like a painter's dying wish. We stand in silence for a long moment until the Ringmaster's baffled laughter bellows out over the city.

"I can't believe Mal lied to me," he says.

"Why did he?"

"I'm not sure. Maybe he wanted this view to himself." He laughs again, tipping his hat at me. "I must be losing my touch."

We take another moment to appreciate the city's beauty and are about to return to the circus when something on the ground catches my eye. I bend down and run my finger along a rock. Standing again, I hold my hand up to the light and stare at the dark stain on the tip of my finger.

"What the hell?"

The Ringmaster leans in close and slowly shakes his head in disbelief. "Blood," he confirms. "See if you can find any more. My eyes aren't what they used to be."

I bend over again and begin searching the ground and quickly find more drops, leading to the edge of the cliff and down a rough patch into the darkness below. I point it out to the Ringmaster, afraid to say anything in case he decides to travel farther into the foreboding shadows.

"Good job," he says. "Let's go."

I stifle an exhausted moan and lead him down the treacherous path, following the trail of blood and feeling nearly overwhelmed by the fear of where it will lead us.

The moon helps a little bit as I push through the thicket but the trees overhead grow denser and denser, making it difficult to track the splotches of blood, though they're admittedly getting larger the farther we go. At length, we reach the bottom of the hill but the path continues on. I halt and look back at the Ringmaster but he just nods, implying that I should keep on going.

"What if an animal is hurt? This is your chance to get on Mal's good side," he says with a smile.

"Great," I mumble and continue on, pushing thorny branches away from my face. Just as I'm about to turn around and explain that I'm tired, grumpy, and in pain, I push through into a clearing, brightly lit by the large moon overhead. The beauty of the clearing wipes the complaints from my mind. There's something dazzling about the simplicity of it after trudging through a half-mile of unforgiving forest. The Ringmaster seems equally impressed because he removes his top hat and leans back against a tree, a bemused look on his face.

"I can't believe—" I start to say but his raised eyebrows silence me. He lifts a finger to his lips to further quiet me and then uses the same finger to point out across the clearing. Looking over, I see a figure pacing relentlessly in a circle around the clearing's perimeter. I squint to make out who it is and finally realize that it's Jayson, the Sword Eater, who swings his weapon recklessly as he walks, mumbling loudly to himself.

The Ringmaster and I stand our ground as he comes nearer, the sword slashing dangerously through the air. His eyes sweep over us but don't seem to focus and he passes on, his blade coming uncomfortably close to me as he makes his way around the perimeter once more, talking to himself incoherently.

"Come on," the Ringmaster instructs, and we follow Jayson, far enough behind to avoid being struck by his weapon.

"...open myself up," he is saying as we move in as close as possible. "I can open myself up, and I can accept, accept the feel of the metal, and avoid cutting myself in half, but it's the other part I can't handle, I can't handle it!" He holds the sword up in front of his eyes. "Every time, I feel like you're going to crush me. And I deserve it!" he cries, tears falling down his face. "I deserve it."

At that moment, he twirls the sword at blinding speed and slashes his own palms, the weapon dancing from hand to hand with a dexterity that astonishes me. Blood gushes out and wets the hilt. Instinctually, I move forward to help him but the Ringmaster holds me back, shaking his head solemnly.

The Sword Eater presses on and we follow, his blood sticking first to the ground and then to our shoes. As he walks and mumbles, he adds more cuts to his palms and the blood flows freely. He continues to rant and even begins to laugh through his tears, a sound that chills me.

After making our way completely around the circle, the Sword Eater abruptly ceases talking and veers to his left, walking to the center of the clearing.

For a moment, we are all still. I try to get the Ringmaster's attention but his eyes are riveted on his performer. Then the Sword Eater raises the weapon above his head and turns the bloody hilt around so that the blade is facing downward toward his upturned eyes. For a moment, I think he'll swallow it, like usual, and then acknowledge our presence, admitting to some kind of practical joke, along with Mal and perhaps even the Ringmaster. But that moment passes.

"I'm ready," he whispers, the sword trembling above him. "I'm ready to be punished for what I did." The blade inches closer and closer to his mouth but fear registers in his eyes now, a fear I've never seen in the dozens of times he's performed this trick in the big top. As the tip of the sword touches his lips, his entire body begins to convulse, the weapon shaking dangerously in his grasp, and with that, he collapses with a cry of pain onto the blood-spattered earth. The sword falls from his hand and lands soundlessly next to its owner.

And then his eyes snap onto mine and the strangled voice that comes from his mouth makes me step back in fear.

"Help me!" he shrieks at us, "Please! There's not enough weight but if you both... walk on me, God damn it! Crush me!" He pushes his body down but there's nowhere else for him to go. Spittle drips from his outstretched tongue and blood drops from his splayed fingers. I feel an urge to step on his face and put him out of his misery but as I move forward, the Ringmaster reaches out and holds me back. I look up and he simply shakes his head again, and then moves away, back toward the path from which we had emerged.

With the Ringmaster's back to me, I step forward and raise my foot over the Sword Eater's face. He looks at me with an expression of sickening gratitude. My foot wavers for a second but then I withdraw it from above his head. His eyes plead with me but I walk away.

The Ringmaster has already vanished into the forest and just as I'm about to enter its darkness, too, a flash of light behind me causes me to stop momentarily. I turn around and what I see pulls the breath from my body.

The Magician stands over the Sword Eater, looking down with compassion. As I regain my breath, I'm about to shout out to him but something stops me. I feel shame and hate myself for it.

I watch as the Magician reaches down and carefully pulls the Sword Eater to his feet. Chris' eyes suddenly lock onto mine as he hugs the broken man strongly. The Sword Eater bursts into tears, though his arms remain at his sides. I feel tears starting to fill my eyes, too, but then, without warning, both men disappear in a shocking, silent puff of smoke.

CANTO TWENTY-FOUR

By the time I reach the hill that leads back up to the circus, I'm surprised to find the Ringmaster already at its peak, staring down at me with an impatient look on his face. The incline looks much steeper from the bottom and I suddenly realize just how tired I really am. It's practically morning and I've been up all night. The incident with Hope and her creepy brother seems like weeks ago. I put my palms on my knees for a second and then shout up the hill.

"Do you know if there's another way around?"

"I took a quick look while I was waiting for you," he shouts down, sounding a little irritated. "Looks like this is it, so start climbing."

Cursing under my breath, I begin clambering up the hillside. I can feel his eyes on me as I puff my way up, cutting my fingers on sharp rocks and occasionally slipping, losing my balance and falling back down several feet at a time. After one particularly bad cut on my hand, I sit down on a large rock, also nursing a stitch in my side. I look up and see the annoyance in the Ringmaster's eyes and my own anger wells up.

"I'm going back down to see if there's another way around."

"Get on your feet and climb! I don't have all day."

"Listen—"

"You listen!" he shouts. The rage in his voice silences me. "I agreed to take you along that night in Boston. Do you think you're the first whiny brat who's ever had that idea?"

And he turns his back on me and strides out of my line of sight. I curse him again but know he's right. I mumble incoherently as I climb, mostly to distract myself from the burning sensation in my legs as the hill grows steeper and the rocks dig deeper into my hands. The voice of my brother echoes in my head now, reminding me that I'm a failure, and it's this ghost that pushes me up over the top, where I fall to the ground, breathing violently but with an insane smile on my face.

When I open my eyes, the Ringmaster's hand is proffered out to me and I take it. He raises me to my feet, a closed-mouth smile matching my own.

"Look, I'm—" I start, but he silences me with a wave of his hand.

"You don't have to say anything. I know how hard this has been, Daniel. And I'm proud of you."

Dawn breaks against the sky like a fugitive from shackles and I smile deliriously as we find a new path. It leads us partially around the circus and I take the time to enjoy the sounds of morning. Eventually, we cross a makeshift bridge and find ourselves staring down at the clearing, signs of life just starting to appear. Van, the Trickster, is already out and is shuffling a deck of cards on his knees as he sits on a boulder. The workers mill about, some running to get started at their jobs, but one person in particular draws my attention. It's the Snake Charmer, and even at this early hour, she's wrapped in a frightening array of serpents. She approaches the Trickster. The Ringmaster and I make our way down the slope and head over to the boulder, too, curious to see this particular freak out in the open so early in the day. The Snake Charmer is infamously adverse to socializing with others, and to sunlight, too, it has seemed. The Trickster puffs incessantly at his always-present cigarette as the three of us converge from different angles. He pretends not to notice us but I can see his eyes move slightly as he picks us up in his peripheral vision.

I reach into my pocket and withdraw the dollar bills I stole from the bike what seems like centuries earlier. The Snake Charmer stares at me with a look of terrifying curiosity.

"I'd like to play, if it's not too early," I hear myself say.

"Never too early," the Trickster replies without looking up. His smoke rises up into my face but I refuse to cough, though my throat burns ferociously. A crowd begins to gather as he counts my money and mumbles, "That'll give you four chances. Sure you want to spend all your money in one place, kid?" Even this early, he's in costume with pristine makeup. The crowd presses closer. I lose sight of the Ringmaster and become increasingly aware of the Snake Charmer, who's right behind me, and I wonder if I'll be bitten while playing this stupid game.

Smiling, the Trickster quickly stands up and crouches behind the boulder, placing the stacked and crumpled bills next to the cards. He then takes the deck into his hand and withdraws three cards, showing them to the audience: three aces, all but the heart. These three cards are placed on the boulder and suddenly they and his hands are moving at blinding speed. An excited murmur echoes through the crowd. No one has ever beaten him. Yes, sometimes he makes an exception for a pretty girl during a show or when the Ringmaster forces him to lose to a particularly sad child, but never to another performer. It's something he takes great pride in, much to the annoyance of some and disgruntled respect of the rest.

He briefly shows me the ace of spades, indicating that it'll be the card to follow. Then the three cards begin their rapid dance. But this time I don't even bother to watch the cards. I watch his hands with a bemused detachment. And when he stops moving the cards, I select one arbitrarily: wrong, clubs. And one of the dollar bills disappears into his pocket. And again the cards blur but I keep my eyes on his hands.

Three more times I guess and I'm wrong, wrong, wrong. A disappointed sigh emanates from behind me.

"Give me one more shot," I request.

"Yeah, right," he scoffs, placing the last of the stolen bills into his pocket. "Anyone else feel like wasting their money?"

Another collective murmur floats up and above the crowd

but no one steps forward, until I feel several small scaly bodies pushing past me. I recoil and watch as the Snake Charmer places a dollar onto the boulder, a python moving up her arm and looping around her shoulder. If the proximity of the reptiles frightens the Trickster, he makes no indication of it.

The cards dance once again and the Snake Charmer's eyes strain desperately, and futilely, to track the chosen ace. At length, the Trickster's fingers slow and the three cards remain motionless and face-down on the rock.

"Well, which one's yours, pretty lady?" the Trickster asks, his contempt for the freak barely concealed. As she stares at the cards, I get my first good look at her and realize that she is, in fact, not at all pretty. I've only seen her through the freak show corridor glass and now, up close, she looks old and tired, and seems to have lived a hard life. The wrinkles beneath the makeup are deep and the circles under her eyes are among the darkest I've ever seen.

She holds out her finger first above one card and then another, and then she finally chooses the third, uncertainty blazing in her eyes. The Trickster flips the card for her, revealing the ace of diamonds. I step forward.

"Ahh, tough luck, sweetie," the Trickster laughs.

As he pulls the card away, my hand lashes out and grips his other wrist, the partially closed left one, and squeezes. Everyone is shocked at my blatant act of aggression, including me. Somewhere nearby, I hear the Ringmaster chuckle.

"Get off me!" the Trickster shouts.

In response, I twist his hand and he shrieks like I did when Ben shoved me into the lockers on my birthday. Just as the last of my strength fades, his fist opens, a fourth card tumbling out and falling face up onto the ground: an extra ace of diamonds.

"Bullshit!" someone behind me yells. I let go and smile maliciously at the Trickster, finally redeemed for the money he tricked me out of the night I first visited the circus. Someone pats me on the shoulder and I look away for a moment to see who it is, but not before another person shouts, "Look out!" Whirling around, I find myself staring at the Trickster's oncoming fist. I brace myself for yet another blow from one of the circus's performers but it never comes. Instead, one of the snakes lashes out and bites the Trickster on the neck, hard, causing his fist to miss me by inches.

He screams in fear and pain, and falls backward onto the ground, his cigarette flying into the air and then down onto his costume. I guess his outfit must be particularly flammable because the fire breaks out almost instantaneously and his screams increase.

"Help! Help me!"

The people he's been cheating out of a dollar here and a dollar there for years simply watch as he rolls around in the dirt, finally managing to put the flames out, tearing his costume to shreds in the process. After a moment, he sits up and fixes the Snake Charmer with a vicious glare.

"Don't worry," she says in some strange accent, the first time I've ever heard her speak. "That one isn't poisonous. I think."

As laughter bubbles up from the dispersing crowd, he turns his gaze on me.

"You. You ruined me. If it's the last thing I do, you'll pay for this."

CANTO TWENTY-FIVE

"**R**elax, Van," the Ringmaster says, seeming to appear from nowhere.

But the Trickster is up in a flash, pushing past my mentor and lunging at me. I move out of the way just in time and the smoldering man runs into the Snake Charmer, the serpents snapping at him viciously. He bats them away, shrieking, and curses her and the Ringmaster, backing away in frenzied hysteria. He surveys us all from a safe distance and then abruptly grabs his crotch in a pathetic stance of defiance.

"Fuck this place!" he screams, and then runs off. I wonder if he'll show up in the corridor tonight, acting like nothing happened.

The few remaining people pat me on the back, saying it's about time that someone put the Trickster in his place. This is the first time I've felt even vaguely accepted by them. But the compliments are short-lived and soon enough, I'm alone by the boulder with the Ringmaster and the Snake Charmer.

"Daniel," she says suddenly, the accent surprising me again. "Would you like to come to my trailer for breakfast?"

After everything that's happened last night and this morning, I realize that I'm incredibly hungry.

"Absolutely."

"You two have fun," the Ringmaster says, distracted. "I have some things to take care of before tonight's show." And with that, he walks off, leaving me alone with the Snake Charmer and her disturbing collection of pets.

Her trailer is clean but cluttered. Piles of miscellaneous stuff and boxes create a virtual maze inside the small space but also add a comfortable air to it. As I close the door behind me, she releases the snakes from her body and they quickly slither off into the shadows. I work hard to suppress a shudder.

"How many snakes do you have?" I ask, nervous, looking around but unable to see any of them anymore.

"Only five," she answers as she lights the stove, heads to the mini-fridge, and cracks a half-dozen large and oddly-colored eggs into a pan. I'm afraid to ask what kind of eggs. "Most snake charmers have at least a dozen but these are the same five I've had for years and we work very well together. None of them have ever bit me." She taps her knuckle briefly against a wooden cutting board.

As she cooks, I take a seat at the small kitchen table.

"I'm sorry about Alicia," she says quietly. "I knew her for a while, not very well of course, but I could tell she really cared about you."

"Thanks," I mumble.

As the eggs bubble, she grabs a stick of incense and lights it from beneath the pan. A beautiful scent quickly rises, commingling with the aroma of the cooking food.

"Where are you from?" I ask after an extended moment of silence.

"Hungary," she replies proudly, flipping the eggs with an expert movement of her muscled arm. "I came here about ten years ago, hoping to marry a rich American. But..." She points at her face. There's no remorse in the smile that appears.

She cuts the eggs in half and places each portion onto mismatched plates, and sets them on the table. Sitting down, she hands me a fork and we both eat in silence for a little while. They're delicious.

"I want to thank you for what you did with Van. He's been stealing from everyone for as long as I can remember but no one could figure out how. It took a small boy to discover the Trickster's trick."

She laughs at her own joke and I decide to disregard my annoyance at being called a "small boy."

"Are you thirsty?" she asks. I nod and she stands, moving leisurely to the refrigerator and withdrawing a glass pitcher of brown liquid. She pours a single cupful and watches as I nervously drink.

It's a weird, spicy mixture, unlike anything I've ever had before, and I love it. I finish it all and smack my lips when I'm done, without embarrassment.

She seems satisfied by this but doesn't offer to refill the glass, much to my disappointment.

"Did you know that Alicia had a sister?" she asks. I nod, wiping my mouth with a sleeve. "Yes, well, I had a sister, too. Agnes. She was a thief, like Van, which drove me mad. She was older than me but even I knew what she did was wrong. We were very little girls, younger than you, and she would steal from our parents' friends. And as she got older, I watched as she would seduce the boys in our classes and then steal from them, too. She would change her personality to fit whichever situation would help make her the most money. Ridiculous! And the more she did it, the better she got at it.

"Finally, she decided she could make even more money in America, so she ran away from home, and broke my parents' hearts. They pleaded for me to find her, so I worked and worked until I had enough money saved and I came to America, too, and searched for my sister, even though I secretly hated her. It was for my parents that I did this thing.

"I found her in New York City shortly after I arrived there. Or, to say better, I found what was left of her. She was killed by a man she had tried to steal from after having sex with him in the bathroom of a bar. And I hated myself then because I was so happy that she was dead and that I was free of my parents and of Hungary and—"

But at that moment, a sound disturbs her story, drawing her attention away from me. In a corner lit by sunlight from a nearby window, two snakes are wrapped around each other, coiling their bodies violently, teeth bared. Remembering Cal's words, I watch in fascination for a long moment and then look up at the Snake Charmer, who's watching me with a smile on her face.

"Are they fighting? Or—" the words seem to freeze on my tongue but I force them out—"having sex? I mean, if they're fighting, shouldn't we stop them?" As if I have any idea how to stop fighting snakes.

The Snake Charmer's smile widens and I feel myself blushing. She leans in close and I can smell the eggs on her breath.

"It doesn't matter what they are doing, Daniel. Sex and war are one and the same, and they lead inev— What is the word? Yes, inevitably to the same conclusion.

"Death."

CANTO TWENTY-SIX

On our last night in Mobile, I sit reading a comic book in the Ringmaster's trailer, the show a distant roar, trying to absorb the words and pictures, but really just looking forward to our next stop: New Orleans. My brother once told me that girls in New Orleans will expose themselves for no reason at all. But my brother often lied when it came to such unbelievable things in life, so I try to keep myself fairly pessimistic about the prospects of naked women, attempting instead to focus on the brightly-clad super-powered misfits beating the shit out of each other.

A sudden knock at the door pulls me away from the comic, which I drop to the floor on my way to see who's visiting. I'm shocked speechless when I see that it's Peter Alpe, the Owner of the circus, who I last saw wrestling with Pietro the Clown. A lit cigar dangles from his fingers.

"Who are you?" he slurs, and I quickly notice that his eyes are bloodshot and his clothes deeply wrinkled.

"I'm... uh... the Ringmaster's assistant."

He grunts and pushes past me and collapses onto one of the flimsy folding chairs, the smell of liquor nearly flattening me. I remain by the door, wondering if I'll be physically attacked yet again in what I now consider my home. "Where's the Ringmaster?" he says.

"He's at the show... y'know... ringmastering."

He shakes his head at this.

"Of course, the show. Jesus." He looks up at me and tries to focus his eyes, to make sense of what's happening, but apparently fails. He looks down at the floor and sways, nearly falling out of the chair. "Got anything to drink here?"

"Sure," I answer and quickly make my way to the mini-fridge, pouring him a glass of juice. I bring it to him and he takes a deep gulp and then sputters, almost spitting it back out all over me. I move back to the door.

"What the hell is this?" he demands.

"Um... juice?"

"Don't you have any liquor?"

"I... don't think so."

"Fine," he concedes and finishes the rest of the juice in a single swallow. Drops of the amber liquid run down his unshaven chin and neck, into the dirty collar of his once-white dress shirt. His tie is ripped in several places.

An awkward moment of silence fills the trailer.

"So—"

"My wife left me," he interrupts, still not looking at me. The warbled sounds of the circus cascade out to us and I place my hand on the door handle, ready for this distraught, drunk businessman to attack me at any moment.

"I'm sorry to hear that," I lie.

"Left me for my financial advisor. My fucking financial advisor!" he yells, throwing the glass against the wall, shattering it, drops of juice splashing across the chipped paint like blood splatter. "And you know what's ironic, Dave?"

"Dan."

"I was working with that prick to get her out of my will before I dumped her!" He bursts out in laughter, once again nearly toppling out of the chair. He rights himself as the laughter fades, transforming into sobs, and I watch with disturbing detachment as Mr. Alpe breaks down into tears, the snot freely running from his nose.

"And they took my money. All of it. I'm worthless now. All I have left is this piece of shit circus. I mean, who the hell even goes to the circus anymore?" He looks up. "Are you *listening* to me?"

I open the door slightly. He stands and I open it a little more, ready to bolt. But he holds his arms up as a peace offering.

"I'm sorry," he says quietly and then sits back down. Several fireflies sneak into the trailer as I stand there with the door open, waiting to see what Alpe will do next. I have to decide whether to make a break for it or stay and listen to a story from yet another messed up adult.

I close the door and lean against the wall, pitying the man against my better judgment.

"When I got home from my office, after I found out about my wife and... you know... some of the kids on my street came up to me while I was unlocking my own God damn front door. They told me that they'd seen her leaving, her and 'some guy' taking stuff from the house and putting it in the back of a nice car, and driving off in a hurry. And these kids, these kids who I've always been such a jerk to, they were so concerned about me. They acted like it was them that got betrayed. And you know what I did? Instead of thanking them or hugging them or whatever?"

The fireflies circle his head.

"I went fucking ballistic!" he yells, swatting at the insects. "I screamed at them, I grabbed their bikes and threw them into the street, I threatened to kill them if they ever came near me again." Tears fall down his face. "I felt like an animal. Like some kind of God damn bear, completely out of control, like something that just needs to be put out of its fucking misery...

"And I think... I think I freaked out at them because they were kids. Frances always wanted a baby but I refused. Too busy, too much going on, too distracted for that kind of bullshit. And look at me now..." He holds up his tie and stares at the ripped material. "It's just not worth it."

He swats again at the fireflies, which seem obsessed with the broken man wearing a thousand dollar suit and sitting on a cheap folding chair. Ash from his cigar falls to the carpet. I rummage around the trailer for an ashtray.

"I'm tired," he says, rubbing his face, his hand sticky with snot and tears. "So tired."

"When's the last time you slept?" I venture, finding a smiley-face ashtray and placing it on a small table in front of Peter. He places his cigar into it without looking down.

"I haven't slept in days. Well, except for a quick nap this morning. I was trying to read the paper and have some breakfast, and I just passed out with my head on the table, half a bite of toast in my mouth. And I had this dream... this crazy dream. I was on a boat, sailing past a land mass that I didn't recognize at all, and I was trying to get home to Frances. And I was close, and I knew I was close, even though the land wasn't familiar. I was about to get there, when suddenly I hit something hard, a rock I think, and the ship began to sink. And all I could think about was Frances, getting home to Frances, and even as the water closed in around me and the darkness covered me, I still thought that somehow I might make it home to her.

"But then the light was gone."

"Maybe you should crash here for a little bit," I offer. "I'll go tell the Ringmaster and I'm sure he can help."

"No," he says, standing abruptly and striding over to me, scattering the fireflies across the trailer. He grabs me by the shoulders roughly but somehow I know that he won't hurt me. "Not the Ringmaster. I need the Tattooed Man."

"What?" I say, trying to shake free and failing. "Why the hell do you need him?"

"I just do. He's always been there for me. I can't explain."

"Well, he hasn't been around much lately."

"I know!" he shouts, letting me go and making his way to my cot, dropping down onto it unceremoniously. I want to tell him to get off but decide he's been through enough already. A firefly lands on his shoulder but he doesn't seem to notice. "I went to his trailer before coming here," he says through an arm that covers his face, "but the door was locked and no one answered when I knocked."

"Look," I say, wanting out of here, "you try to get some sleep and I'll go see if I can track him down. I'm friends with the Snake Charmer, and she might know where he is. Okay?"

But his eyes are closed, his chest moving up and down rhythmically. Several more fireflies land on him and pulse in time with his breathing.

I shake my head at this bizarre sight and then leave the trailer, closing the door quietly behind me.

CANTO TWENTY-SEVEN

I've learned during my several months in the circus that the Tattooed Man's real name is Monty, but don't know much else about him. He's been noticeably absent from the freak show in recent weeks. At first, he made sporadic appearances until eventually he stopped showing up at all. The Ringmaster attempted to contact him about his absence but told me that every time he visited the trailer, Monty was nowhere to be found.

I approach his door as the sounds of that night's performance echo behind me. I hesitate before knocking—what am I doing here?—but then I remember Peter's slumped form in the Ringmaster's trailer. Releasing a resigned sigh, I knock on the flimsy trailer door and wait.

Nothing.

I knock again but there's still no response. My loyalty to the drunken, enraged Owner of the circus fading, I turn to leave but then decide to give it one more try. I rap on the door a third time, harder now, and call out to the Tattooed Man, doubting he can hear me but trying anyway.

"Monty? It's Dan. Mr. Alpe asked me to stop by. His... uh... his wife just left him for his... financial guy, and now he's passed out drunk in the Ringmaster's trailer. He's... uh... not doing so well."

Nothing.

Frustrated and annoyed, I turn away from the door again

and I'm two steps down the trailer's stairs when I hear the door unlock behind me. I turn and once again mount the steps, entering the Tattooed Man's home.

In my entire life, I have never seen a place in worse shape. Furniture has been ripped apart (apparently by hand), food and drink are spilled in every crevice imaginable, and it reeks of urine and feces. In the corner, a makeshift fireplace has been created, with a dented, dilapidated metal chute rising up and out of the ceiling, where a tattered hole has been ripped open with some kind of blunt instrument. In front of the small but roaring fire is the only untouched piece of furniture: a beautiful, antique chair. A man... Monty, I assume... sits in it with his back to me. His bald head reflects the fire's light.

"Come in," he intones, even though I'm already inside. I leave the door open in case I needed to get the hell out of there in a hurry. I stand there in silence for a moment, trying to figure out how he managed to unlock the door then get back into his chair so quickly.

"Well, whaddaya waitin' for?" he asks, coughing his last words and spitting phlegm into a handkerchief. "Come over here and I'll tell you all about Mister Alpe."

I approach the chair at an oblique angle, making sure to stay far enough away that he can't grab me. He's always made me nervous and no more so than now. I nearly trip over a broken piece of couch as Monty comes into full view.

He is swathed completely in heavy, wool blankets despite the prodigious heat from the small fire. Every part of his body is covered except his head, which sweats profusely. His face is deeply flushed and I can tell that its redness isn't only from the fire. He's sick, very sick, and I take an additional step away from him, nearly bumping into the wall. The red of his face almost disguises his similar-colored birthmark that covers his cheeks and nose, but I can still make out its muddled contours.

"If you're gonna stare, might as well have a seat."

I lean back against the wall and slide down until I'm seated on the floor amid the detritus that is his trailer.

"When I was your age, I didn't have any friends either." I start to protest but he silences me with a look: I know he's right and he knows that I know. "But at least I had an excuse. This is the face that launched a thousand shits! Heh." He coughs again into his discolored handkerchief. "I hated my face, hated myself, and pretty much everyone else, too. And when I got old enough, I decided to have surgery, to get rid of these ugly-ass splotches, to just be a regular guy. And as I was sittin' in the doctor's office, gettin' stared at by all the 'normal' people in the waiting room, I realized that I didn't want to be anything like them. I realized that they were stupid and boring, and that my face was a gift from God to keep me separated from them."

I shift uncomfortably on the garbage-strewn floor.

"I started getting tattoos pretty soon after that. At first, I got ones that matched my face and that led to other ones, crazier ones, and I started getting addicted to it: the pain, the healing, the way they looked on top of my muscles. But it got harder and harder to keep a job, let alone get one.

"So, one day I'm waiting to get another tattoo done, when I realize I'm sittin' across from some joker in a business suit. Totally out of place. He musta caught me starin' at him cuz he starts talking to me, tellin' me how cool my tats are. Turns out he's there cuz his wife is in back gettin' one herself... a butterfly on her back, right above her ass.

"Typical, right?"

I don't have an answer for him.

"Anyway, we get to talkin' and I realize that this guy, who turned out to be Peter, obviously, is pretty fuckin' cool. He owned a bunch of businesses, including the circus, which is especially cool. And the thing is... I hated everyone, including him at first, but then I realized that Peter hated everyone too, except maybe his wife.

"Peter and I became friends and he invited me to join the freak show. If anyone else had said that, I'd beat the shit out of them, but I knew there was no malice from him, just business, pure and simple. And we've been good friends for years, even though we don't really tell anyone in the circus about it. I mean, it's not really any of their fuckin' business, you know?

"But things changed recently. Didja hear about that fight between Peter and that clown Pietro?"

"I saw it."

"You saw it? Shit, I wish I had seen that. Sounded awesome.

"Anyway, like I was saying, a few days after that fight, Frances showed up here at my trailer. She and I have never really talked much... I always kinda suspected that she was only with Peter for the money. So, she shows up at my trailer and she's with Peter's financial advisor, which I didn't really get at first. I thought maybe they were planning a surprise birthday party for him or something. But they told me they were running away together. I couldn't figure out why they were telling me but it didn't matter. I cursed them out and told them I was gonna tell Peter everything. And then...

"And then, just like that, she was kissing me... even with the way I look... her hands all over me, with that financial guy sitting in this chair and just watching. The thing is... the thing is that I always secretly wanted Frances and I think... I think she knew that cuz she said a lot of things over the years to me that seem different now, thinking back on it. And I guess some part of her wanted Peter's freak friend, too. And clearly both she and the financial guy are freaks on some level because she seduced me right then and there, with that weird financial douche bag sitting in this chair and watching, laughing every once in awhile.

"I've never felt so powerless. I was so happy and so miserable at the same time, ya know? I knew they were doing this just to destroy Peter, make him think that even a tattooed freak is better than him. And yet I promised I wouldn't tell and they left, the both of them still laughing. And I didn't tell Peter. I kept that promise."

"Why?"

He looks at me with a hatred that chills me even in the heat of the trailer.

"Because I was waiting for her to come back. I thought we connected while we were together, even for those few minutes... I thought she realized that we're meant for each other. But I was wrong. I'm just a freak to her, just a story they can laugh about after they disappear." He giggles at this thought but it turns into coughing, which lasts for nearly a full minute. He spits into his handkerchief and then stares at the mucous-filled rag for a second before throwing it into the fire, where it ignites after a moment and soon vanishes in blackness.

"Are you sick?" I venture.

"Very fuckin' perceptive, Dan. No wonder the Ringmaster likes you. Heh. Yeah, I'm sick all right. About a week after Frances fucked me, I went to a doctor in Georgia. He told me that I've contracted leprosy somehow, probably from a dirty tat needle. How hilarious is that?"

"Leprosy?"

"Yeah, it's a skin disease, dipshit. Pretty rare, too, which is even funnier. It basically rots you from the outside in. I'm cold as hell lately. Can't seem to ever get warm enough."

"Shouldn't you, y'know, be in a hospital or something?"

He laughs again, derisive and dismissing. "Nah, why bother? I'm falling apart no matter what. Get it? Ha! So I might as well stay in my home. Or what passes for a home.

"And you know what the worst part is? I still think that Frances might come back. Hell, when you knocked, I hoped at first that it was her. That's what a fuckin' moron I am."

Silence fills the trailer. Outside, it sounds like the performance is finishing up and I realize I need to get back to my trailer. At that moment, Monty leans forward and holds out his arms toward the fire. At first, it looks like his skin is melting from the intense heat but then I realize that it's his disease-ravaged flesh. I can still make out a few distended tattoos in the fire's uneven light.

On his right palm is an incredibly detailed green lion; on the back of his left hand, a stern-looking eagle. On his right forehand, a blue lion stares out from a white background.

"I haven't left the trailer since I was diagnosed," he says, turning toward me. Swallowing nervously, I slowly get to my feet, ready to go. I lose my balance for a second and start to pitch forward slightly.

"Oh, one more thing, Dan..." he says, and is suddenly up out of the chair, his naked arms wrapping around me. "Leprosy is contagious. Heh."

I struggle to free myself but he lets go, laughing and returning to his chair. I explode out of the door, disgusted. The sound of dozens of car engines starting echoes in the distance.

I enter my trailer and see that Peter is still passed out on the cot. The fireflies are gone. I desperately want to shower but suddenly realize that Peter's cigar is smoldering in the ashtray and I curse myself for not putting it out before I left to check on the Tattooed Man. I quickly walk over and stub the cigar out. Peter sighs and mumbles something in his sleep, and I can suddenly see the child this wealthy man once was. I pull my blanket up and over his body and, as I do so, he wakes briefly, though his eyes barely open.

"Hey... Dan... did you find him?"

I stare at his heavy eyelids for a second before answering, "No. Sorry."

He sighs again and turns over, away from me and toward the wall. I hurry into the bathroom, eager to shower, acutely aware of the ghost of Monty's deteriorating limbs on my body.

CANTO TWENTY-EIGHT

I strip out of my clothes in record time and jump into the shower, not even waiting for the water to heat up. I scrub my body mercilessly but can't seem to free myself from the Tattooed Man's lingering touch. I'm lathering my face for the third time when the lights suddenly go out. The soap stings my eyes bitterly as I fumble with the showerhead, trying to clear my face, shut off the water, and get out of the stall at the same time.

Out in the main part of the trailer, which is also dark, Peter Alpe has vanished. Shivering, with only a towel around my waist, I peer out a window and see that all of the circus's electricity is gone. Adding to my confusion, I can hear people shouting indiscriminately in the distance, though I can't make out any words, only panicked bursts of raw emotion. I'm baffled by how a circus-wide blackout can have occurred. The Ringmaster and his technical crew are meticulous about the generators and never allow anyone else anywhere near them.

I dress quickly and bolt out of the trailer, desperate for answers and ready to forget the incident at Monty's. At first, I don't see anyone but as I make my way closer to the big top, shadows begin to rush past me, both human and animal, and I have to move quickly to avoid being knocked over. I attempt, futilely it turns out, to stop someone and find out what's happening. I can make out snippets of half-shouted conversations; something has definitely happened to the generators; not one, but all of them.

As I reach the top of the hill that leads down to the big top, a form staggers up and haltingly approaches me. The clouds move past the moon and I find myself staring at Delores, the Acrobat, with whom I've spoken little since our trip to Lance and Hugh's place, way back in Providence.

"Delor—" I start but the words dry up in my throat as I realize she's holding something against her stomach. No, not against. In. She's attempting to hold her guts in her stomach. A vicious cut runs across her abdomen, blood and intestines and God knows what else spilling through her stained fingers. I begin running to her, screaming her name, when I catch movement in my peripheral vision.

I've barely turned my head when a baby elephant charges into me, both of us blind with fear, and as I tumble to the ground beneath its cute but deadly hooves, sparks explodes behind my closed eyes and I ready myself to be trampled to death by the least likely member of the circus.

I must have blacked out for a few minutes because when I wake up, there's a deep gash in my left cheek and Delores is no-where to be seen. Making my way groggily to my feet, I stumble down the hill and stand in front of the freak show corridor, trying to find someone, anyone, but I can only hear the distant cries of animals.

A pair of hands abruptly grabs me and swings me around, away from the corridor. It's Mr. Atlantis and this is the first time I've ever seen fear on his face.

"Dan, what the hell are you doing here?"

"I was in the shower and the lights—"

"Never mind that. You should get back to your trailer imme-diately," he says, looking around.

"Wait, what's going on?"

"I don't know. I think someone sabotaged the generators. The Ringmaster is convinced it was one of the performers, someone who's been trying to take the circus down for weeks, maybe even months. People are hurt, that's why you need to—"

"I know! I saw Delores and her stomach is cut up real bad. She needs to get to a hospital!"

"Shit, really? Okay, I'll find her and take care of it. In the meantime, you get yourself back to the trailer and stay there until morning. You got that?"

"Yes," I lie.

Without a further word, he disappears into the darkness. I'm paralyzed for a moment but then decide to jog around the big top and see if I can find and maybe even help Delores.

The sound of high-pitched shrieking reaches me and I head in its direction. But I stop in my tracks when I discover the source: the three female clowns are splayed on the ground, punching and clawing at each other, demonic screams coming from their throats. I can't figure out what would have caused these three to go after each other in such a barbaric fashion but, as I watch them from the shadows, they seem to morph into one terrible person, and I back away from this amalgamation of evil, hoping never to witness such a thing again.

As I continue my way around the big top, to the left, I see a small light approaching me. At first, it looks like a firefly but it grows in size as it comes closer. I quickly realize that it's a pen light, held by none other than Pluto. As I enter his circle of light, a sneer wraps itself around his face and then, curiously, vanishes. In my nervousness, I wipe the blood from my cheek across the rest of my face, making me feel like some kind of war-painted madman. We stare at each other for a second in the dim glow of his pen light.

"Please, kid," he finally says, surprising me with his choice of words, "I need your help."

"Me?"

"Yeah, I know, you're not my first choice, but you're the only one I can find."

The cut on my cheek is pulsing and I can't find any pity in me for someone who has hated me from the moment we met. I step away from Pluto, disappointment already creasing his face. But just as I ready myself to turn away, I remember the way the Magician stared at me in the forest, just before he vanished with the Sword Eater.

"Okay," I finally say, "What can I do?"

Pluto leads me into the big top using a side-flap that I didn't even know existed. In the small "backstage" area, to which I've never been invited, the Fat Lady is lying in a mound of hay, her face contorted in agony, her breath coming in ragged gasps.

"What's wrong? Is she okay? Is she dying?" I blurt, picturing the gash in Delores's stomach and wondering if she's even still alive.

"No, she ain't dying, you idiot." And then, off my look: "Sorry, habit. No, she's giving birth to a baby. To our baby."

I almost blurt out that I thought she was hooking up with the Fire Eater but realize quickly enough that it would be the absolute worst thing I could say and would solve nothing. Instead: "Wow."

"Yeah, yeah, we're a couple. Big fucking joke, but it's our business so no one knows. Now, here's what I needja to do. I gotta go find that clown, Pietro. I hear he used to be a doctor. I need you to sit with her, hold her hand, tell her I'm gonna be right back and that it's gonna be okay. Can you do that?"

"Y-yeah," I answer, taking her chubby hand in mine.

"Okay, great, thank you." He gets up and walks away but stops just before melting into the shadows. "And don't try anything funny. She's the love of my life." I open my mouth in shock at his statement but he smiles, the only act of kindness I've ever really received from him. And then he's gone.

The Fat Lady moans angrily a moment later and squeezes my hand, and I nearly scream in agony. She is ridiculously strong. I think about wresting my hand from hers but the look of pain on her face is enough to make me accept part of her suffering as my own. Several minutes of this back and forth torment stretch on until her hand suddenly goes slack and falls away from mine. I look up and find her staring into my eyes.

"I know you were there," she whispers.

"What?" I ask, though I know exactly what she's talking about.

"When I was in here... with the... with him," she gasps. "I saw you up in the bleachers after he left. I knew I shouldn't... cry in front of you, in front of anyone... but I was just so devastated."

"I'm sorry," I say quietly.

"Thank you," she replies, touching my cut cheek gently. "Thank you for not saying anything to Gerry. I know he's been terrible to you but it would break his heart if he found out. It was just..." She winces again. "Just a one-time mistake. I love Gerry so much."

I nod and she turns away, grabbing my hand again and

crushing it, a low guttural groan of pain emanating from her mouth.

It seems like an eternity passes before Pluto finally returns, via the side-flap, with Pietro in tow. I can smell the liquor on the Clown's breath but Pluto doesn't seem to care.

"Okay, here she is," the Midget proclaims, standing with his hands outstretched, eager for the Clown to transform into a doctor.

"Yes, yes," Pietro says, dropping his medical kit onto the hay and rummaging around inside. He withdraws rubber medical gloves and puts them on slowly, apparently out of practice.

"Are you sure you're up for this?" I ask.

"What?" he shouts, as if realizing for the first time that I'm there. "Are you kidding me? I was in the top of my medical class in Italy before I lost all my money and was forced to move to America! This medical kit was my stepfather's, before he abandoned my mother, my poor mother. She never even-"

"All right, all right," Pluto interrupts, "let's do the soap opera stuff later. Can you help my woman out or what?"

"Well, I should call in some help but apparently the closest hospital is twenty-five miles away and I don't think she can hold on that long, from the looks of things."

As if on cue, the Fat Lady moans loudly and increases the pressure on my hand. I bite the inside of my cheek to avoid crying out. The Clown bends over and lifts her dress. Pluto takes his place on the other side of the Fat Lady and grabs her other hand, sweat dotting his small forehead. A parade of unbearable moist noises rises up from where the Clown is ensconced underneath the Fat Lady's dress. I want to block my ears but I only have one free hand. After several more moments of this, Pietro reappears with a frown on his face.

"What? What is it?" Pluto demands.

"There's a problem. The baby is in breech position and due to the... er... the unique body type of the patient, I'm afraid a regular delivery might be life-threatening for both mother and child."

"Jesus Christ!" Pluto yells.

"But... there's another option," the Clown says quietly. Pluto and I stare at him as the Fat Lady moans. "C-section."

The thought alone nearly makes me vomit. Pluto has no such qualms.

"Do it."

Pietro nods and delves back into his medical kit, withdrawing a syringe and a small bottle of medicine.

"I'm going to give her a local anesthetic. She won't feel a thing but I want you two to keep her mind occupied. I don't need her, or you two for that matter, looking down at what I'm doing and panicking."

"Okay," Pluto says, and I agree.

"Now, Daniel," Pietro continues, "take the pen light from Gerry and shine it on her belly. You don't need to look once it's in the right spot but I might tell you to adjust it accordingly, understand?" I nod, finally releasing her hand, thankfully, and take the light from Pluto. Pietro rips open the dress below her enormous breasts. I hold the light up so that its small glow covers the center of her enormous stomach and then turn my face away. The last thing I see down there is Pietro administering the shot and withdrawing a scalpel from his bag.

As he begins cutting, which I can unfortunately hear in detail, the Fat Lady reaches up and grabs Pluto's hair gently, their eyes locking. As the surgical sounds increase, I struggle to fight back my nausea and hold the light steady at the same time. After a while, I don't really hear anything anymore. Watching the two of them stare at each other, I realize how much they love each other and realize also how much I miss Alicia and Camilla.

The Clown gives me occasional directions regarding the placement of the light, which I must hear on some level, because I comply without even realizing what I'm doing. And the more I stare at the Midget and the Fat Lady, the more surreal the scene becomes. With her hand in his hair and the dim, moving light, it almost appears as if she's holding up his disembodied head, lighting the grisly scene like a jack o'lantern held aloft. I laugh to myself at the thought and then just close my eyes, pretending I can't hear the loud, squishy cutting noises.

I know I don't fall asleep because I perform my light-bearing duties without incident, but the next thing I know, there's a sharp slapping noise and the big top is filled with the sound of a newborn baby's cries.

I open my eyes and find myself staring at a strange new family: the Fat Lady holding the already-quieting baby, a boy; and Gerry, who stands over them with a delirious smile on his face. After taking in the scene for a few moments, I look at the Clown, who's just finishing up a maze of stitches, tears on his face. And before I know it, we're all crying and looking at each other in amazement.

Pietro wipes the tears from his cheeks and approaches me, pulling me up off the ground, and takes me aside.

"I'm very proud of you, Daniel. Not many young men your age could have handled that."

"Thanks."

"Now," he says, breathing out heavily. "I need you to do one more thing for me. She's okay for now, but both she and that baby need to get to a hospital immediately. Do you think you can find someone who can get an ambulance here?"

"Absolutely," I say.

"Good," he replies, patting me on the back.

I steal one last glance at the bizarre family before I exit the big top. Gerry now holds the baby and the Fat Lady stares up at her son and her lover, a look of complete bliss on her chubby face.

CANTO TWENTY-NINE

I find myself sprinting through almost pitch blackness, the sights and sounds of chaos warping around me. Struggling to make out a face I recognize, I pass the latrines and cover my mouth and nose absentmindedly with a hand. Between the darkness and the stench, my senses are severely compromised, which might explain why I run head-first into something... I'm not sure what... but it's something hard and I collapse into a heap, secretly elated to have a chance to rest after the night's histrionics. Unconsciousness envelops me.

It's not quite a dream and not quite a memory. Years earlier, my family had visited my father's cousin, a private pilot who lived from hotel to hotel. His most recent stopover had deposited him a few miles outside of Boston, so we all jammed into the car and headed over. My brother tortured me in the backseat, of course, so fresh tears adorned my face as we pulled up to the hotel. We reached his door and were shocked to find that his room was overrun with ants. He was swearing even as he let us in, cursing the shabby hotel and its "immigrant" manager. My parents assured him that they'd help him secure a new room, so the three of them herded me and my brother to the lobby.

As they shouted at the frightened manager, my brother nodded at the candy machine in an adjacent hallway, so I followed him sheepishly, afraid we might get in trouble for leaving the adults. But if they noticed, they made no indication. They were taking far too much pleasure in hurling racial epitaphs at the shivering man behind the counter.

We approached the machine and I told my brother that I didn't have any money (in fact, he had recently stolen my last dollar but I didn't think any good would come out of mentioning that). He scoffed at me wordlessly and withdrew that same dollar from his pocket. I fought an urge to snatch it and run. He ripped a small hole near the top of the bill and then withdrew a piece of string from the same pocket. Quickly, without even glancing back at our parents, he tied the string onto the dollar, tightened it, and stuck the bill into the machine. It ate the dollar and registered it, but my brother pulled on the string and the dollar popped back out. He selected two fifty-cent candy bars, which fell into the output bin, and he walked away, taking a bite from each, leaving the rigged dollar in my hand.

I looked over as he entered the lobby but my parents were still oblivious to both of us. I swallowed nervously. I was really hungry but I knew this was wrong. My brother never gave me this kind of opportunity, though, and I thought I'd be a fool not to take advantage. Slowly, I placed the bill into the slot, wavering, but then pushed it forward, watching it disappear into the machine. The money registered again and I quickly pulled on the string. But clearly I lacked my brother's technique because it got stuck inside the machine's guts. I pulled desperately, forgetting entirely about the candy, sure that the dollar could be traced directly back to me. As I continued to struggle with the string, a reflection in the machine's glass window caught my eye and I found myself staring at a hotel security guard. I turned, slowly, letting the string go slack and fall from my hand.

"I-"

"Save it," he interrupted. "Follow me."

As I did, my brother watched and laughed from the lobby.

I found out later that my parents were so outraged by my thievery that they decided to leave me unclaimed in the security

office for a few hours, but my father's cousin balked at this cru-
elty and came to collect me about twenty minutes after my in-
carceration. As we walked back to his new room, me trying to
fight back tears and appear tough in front of this distant rela-
tion, he told me to cheer up. He promised that he'd teach me to
fly one day, which was more than enough to clear away some of
the guilt and shame I was feeling.

But I never saw him again after that night. A year later, he
died in a horrific plane crash, killing a family of tourists along
with himself. It turns out he had been flying and instructing
without a valid license.

When I wake up, on the ground, I have no idea how much
time has passed, but it's darker and it sounds like the circus
is still in chaos. My nose is filled with blood and my ears are
strangely blocked, though I can't feel any evidence of blood in
them. My mouth is painfully dry and I try, unsuccessfully, to
conjure up enough saliva to swallow.

I get to my feet, wobbly, my head spinning. Moving forward,
unsure of where the big top is, I call out for help but my voice
sounds weak, especially to my own impaired ears. I walk, partially blind and deaf, yelling in a hoarse voice like a sick animal.

At length, the moon is once again revealed from behind a
blanket of clouds and I realize I'm in a small clearing a ways
away from the circus, on a hill just above the big top. A wave
of dizziness passes over me and I sink to the ground, trying to
stop myself from puking. To take my mind off the overwhelming
nausea and growing headache, I pick at the growing number of
scabs on my face. The dizziness slowly fades and, just as one
of the scabs breaks off onto my fingernail, I hear a low growl
behind me.

Getting slowly to my knees and shifting my vision, I see that
a small lion has emerged from a small cluster of bushes nearby.
It's staring at me and it looks hungry.

The lion pads silently toward me and I hold my breath, hoping that it somehow isn't aware of my presence. A long, excruciating moment stretches on. But the moment passes and a low rumble begins to sound from the lion's throat. It grows louder and the animal's muscles tense and I ready myself once again to die. The lion leaps as its growl reaches its loudest and I force my eyes to remain open, ready to face my death without blinking.

But just as the lion's claws graze my mangled face, a figure comes bursting out of the darkness, tackling the creature and rolling down the embankment with it, hand over paw. I convince myself that my savior must be the Ringmaster or Mr. Atlantis or even the Magician, but as I stare down at the battling forms, I come to realize that it's Mal, the Animal Trainer. At this point, I'm not exactly sure who he's more concerned about; he probably doesn't want the lion to chip a tooth devouring me.

I watch in fascination as they wrestle below me, each struggling for an advantage over the other. At one point, Mal manages to roll behind the lion and get it into a strange headlock. As they rock back and forth in that position, they look almost like spooning lovers, partaking in playful games before a long night's sleep. But this mirage quickly dissipates as the lion frees itself from its master's grip and rolls on top of him, sinking its teeth deep into Mal's shoulder. The Animal Trainer grimaces but doesn't scream. Incredibly, he just grabs the animal's face and pushes it away from the torn flesh.

The lion shoves its face forward but Mal holds onto its maw, keeping it away from his body. This stalemate lasts for several moments until Mal's strength seems to falter. Then, almost as if deciding to give the lion what it wants, Mal lets go and plunges his fist into the animal's throat. Incredulous, I watch as the lion attempts to cough the fist out, to get away from Mal, but the grizzled man stays with the animal, and I realize that the creature can't breathe. After a few more frenzied moments, as Mal attempts to keep the lion from biting down with his free hand, the animal's body goes limp and rolls off of him.

The Animal Trainer pulls his saliva- and blood-covered arm from the lion's mouth and stands up, grasping his mauled shoulder. I stumble down the hill and stare at him in awe.

"Is it... dead?" I ask.

"No way," he spits back, barely looking at me. "I'd rather kill a human than one of my own animals. She's just unconscious for a little while. When she wakes up, she'll be back in her cage with an extra helping of beef for her troubles."

"Are you okay?"

"Yeah, it's just a scratch. I've had worse. Howboutchu? You okay?"

"I'm fine. But the Fat Lady just gave birth and she needs an ambulance right away."

"Birth? What the hell? Wait, I don't even want to know. This place is a freak show. Okay, we can go get help with my car. I should probably get this arm looked at anyway. Let's just stop at my tent for a minute so I can drop her off."

Grunting, he lifts the lion up and throws it over his uninjured shoulder. We walk off, toward his tent, each of us a bloody mess.

"We can discuss a payment plan in the car," Mal says after a moment.

"What payment plan?"

"For saving your life. I promised the Ringmaster I'd look after you but I never said how much it would cost."

The moon falls behind the clouds again but I swear I see a smile cross the old man's face before it vanishes in the darkness.

CANTO THIRTY

By the time we stop by Mal's tent to drop off the lion, grab his car keys, and then head over to the parking lot, dawn is breaking across the sky like a bloody egg in a skillet. It's an ominous sunrise and I remember that this is supposed to be our last day in Mobile.

As we approach the distant line of cars, I'm surprised to find most of the performers gathered there. I look at Mal in confusion but he just shrugs. The Ringmaster sees our approach and separates himself from the others. Mal nods at him and my mentor does the same, and then turns his gaze on me. His eyes run over my bruised and bloody face.

"Are you okay?" the Ringmaster asks.

"I'm fine. It was just... a long night. Is the Fat Lady all right?"

"The ambulance just left with her and Gerry."

"Someone should take a look at Mal. His shoulder—"

But turning to my left, I see that Mal has disappeared, maybe into the crowd, maybe out to his car.

"Mal can take care of himself," the Ringmaster says.

I indicate the gathered crowd and ask him what's going on.

"Charlie just found two people sneaking around. They claim that they're reporters," he answers, pointing toward the center of the crowd, where two black-haired people, an older man and a younger woman, are talking to the Circus Manager. "Apparently they're from the Mobile Register and they heard about the blackout somehow. We're just now getting everything under control, so I haven't had a chance to talk to them yet. Come on."

As if on cue, Charlie calls out to the Ringmaster, beckoning him over. I follow, tired and still a bit dizzy, but curious to see what all the fuss is about. The man, who has deep wrinkles set in his face, reaches out and shakes the Ringmaster's hand.

"Howdy, my name's Adam Gianni and this here is my photographer, Mira. I hear you're more or less the leader around here."

"More or less."

Mira snaps a picture of the Lion Tamer flanked by the three female clowns, who have clearly made up after their frantic brawl earlier this morning.

"So," Adam continues, "can you tell me how this blackout occurred? Is it true that some of your more dangerous animals are still on the loose?"

As the Ringmaster assures Adam that everything is fine, I can tell that he's humoring the reporter and I'm amused by the subtle snide comments that Adam doesn't seem to realize are actually insults directed at him. But my amusement begins to fade as I watch the Ringmaster's eyes and realize that he's also giving silent commands to the performers, who are slowly closing in around the reporter and the photographer. I feel myself backing off, though some primal part of me wants to see how this goes down. Adam doesn't seem to notice the closing circle around him but Mira does and I can see the fear in her eyes. I feel bad for her but also recognize that if I say anything, I might find myself at the center of that circle, too.

Adam is asking what must be his tenth question when the Ringmaster suddenly interrupts him. "I'm sorry but you said you work for the Mobile Register, right?"

"Yep," Adam replies, smiling.

"And this—" pointing at Mira—"is a professional photographer, also hired by the Mobile Register, to get pictures of a blacked-out circus and some dangerous animals?"

"Well, I wouldn't quite put it that way but... yep." A little less confident now, the smile fading.

The top hat's shadow blankets Adam's face and his eyes gloss over.

"I'm sure you two are very close, working together as partners, so why don't you give your photographer a nice, long kiss."

"Kiss?" Adam repeats, his face draining of color.

"Now."

The reporter blinks several times and then turns and grabs Mira, wrapping his arms around her.

"No," she protests quietly. Adam tightens his grip as the denizens of the circus laugh at the spectacle. He pushes his face close to hers, their eyes locking in frenzied desperation. Mira pushes against his chest but he's too strong. As his lips are just about to touch hers, she screams violently at him. "Dad, stop it!"

The crowd goes dead silent as Adam releases his daughter and shakes his head as if coming out of a drug-induced sleep. He blinks rapidly and stares at Mira, a look of horror crossing his face.

Abruptly, he lunges at the Ringmaster, a volley of insults bubbling up from his throat. My mentor watches impartially as Kane appears from nowhere to hold the man back. Adam struggles, futilely, but manages to flail an arm out, striking the Ringmaster in the stomach. My mentor merely smiles and shakes his head as Kane tightens his grip. The three female clowns crowd around Mira, daring her wordlessly to make a move.

"Now," the Ringmaster says, "let's try that again. Who are you really?"

"Fuck you!" Adam yells, bloody spittle flying from his lips.

"We've had a long, long night, Mr. 'Gianni,' and my patience with you is already gone." He covers Adam's face once again in the top hat's shadow. "Who are you?"

The man's face softens; he's easily the most susceptible to the Ringmaster's influence of anybody I've seen.

"My... my name really is Adam Gianni," he gasps and I hear a small sob from Mira. "That's my daughter. Her mom left us years ago."

"You've been following us for a while now. Why?"

"We're from North Carolina. I run a small tabloid there. Maybe you've heard of it, the National Witness? It's pretty much just me and Mira and a few interns. We do a pretty good business but—"

"Get to the point," the Ringmaster orders.

"We... we do good business but not enough. Mira can barely

afford college and I want to give her every opportunity I never had. So, I do some P.I. work on the side, usually real light stuff. But a month or so ago, I got approached by Senator Argent's wife..." The Ringmaster raises his eyebrows at this name. "Yeah, I thought that would get your attention. She came to me with an offer too good to refuse. Everyone knew the Senator was in some kind of accident and that he's been in a coma ever since. But no one knew how or why. His wife told me that she suspected you... that one of your performers was sleeping with his daughter, and when he found out about it... something bad happened."

More titters ripple through the crowd but the Ringmaster silences them with a look.

Adam continues, "She offered me money, a lot of money, to follow you and get proof of what you did, and to sabotage you somehow if I could. Little did I know that there was already someone inside your circus who wants this place destroyed as much as she does."

"Who?" I blurt out.

"I was tired of barely scratching by, making up ridiculous stories about dead rock stars and alien invasions. We were supposed to meet your traitor tonight to discuss how to take you down but the blackout ruined everything. I almost think it's him, double-crossing me."

"Who?" I yell, pushing forward and grabbing Adam's shirt. Kane smiles at my rage.

"Leave him alone, you asshole!" Mira screams at me, struggling to free herself from the giggling clowns. One of them, the shortest, grabs Mira by the hair and pushes her down to her knees, small whimpers bubbling up from her throat. "Please... just leave us alone. We won't bother you anymore."

Several of the performers mock her mewling and I watch in pleasure as the short clown pushes her farther onto the ground. Kane strengthens his grip on Adam and the others circle in closer, smelling blood. I do, too, relishing the prospect of seeing these liars get what they deserve. As Mira sees what's about to happen, she screams, and I feel myself laughing at her helplessness.

"Enough!"

Everyone stops and looks at the Ringmaster. He stands,

enraged, staring at me. Awareness and then shame washes over me. "You, of all people," he whispers, spitting the words. He looks away from me and I step back. The performers wait for the Ringmaster's order.

"Let them go."

"What?" Kane bellows. "You heard them. They're gonna try to bring us down. With a Carnie's help. We gotta beat a name outta them."

"It's not worth it," the Ringmaster replies. "We caught them before any damage was done, and I don't want another coma victim on our collective conscience."

A disgruntled murmur rises from the crowd but they comply, letting go of Adam and his daughter. As the two of them back away from us into the parking lot, Mira stares at me with a hatred that burns into my soul. The vileness of my behavior suddenly hits me and I turn to apologize to the Ringmaster, only to discover that he has already moved off, heading for the trailers. I hurry after him, pushing through the dispersing crowd.

"Hey!" I call out, finally catching up to him. He stops and looks down at me, taking off his top hat. "I... I'm sorry. I don't know what happened back there, but that wasn't me. I guess I... I just got caught up in the moment. I'm really sorry. I know I disappointed you."

To my surprise, a large smile appears on his face. "I know you're sorry, Daniel, which is why I'm not mad. But remember the clearing... remember what happened to the Sword Eater."

He winks at me, replaces the hat on his head, and strides off into the growing sunlight. I stand, watching him, amazed at his words of advice and, even more so, the fact that he hadn't actually been there when I witnessed the Magician's miraculous reappearance and just as sudden vanishing.

I run after him, ready to get a few hours sleep before the last show, and ready also to get the hell out of Alabama.

CANTO THIRTY-ONE

"Where is that fucking nimrod?" Charlie, the Circus Manager, bellows, standing in front of the trucks and trailers, spittle flying from his chapped lips.

We're parked at a rest stop at the top of a hill just off the highway. Several truck drivers decided to pull over while others continues to soldier on ahead of us. Micky, the retarded Talent Scout and Shit Collector, has inexplicably gone missing in the thirty seconds we've been here, and Charlie is furious.

The Ringmaster rolls his eyes as the Manager continues to yell, swiveling his head around in what looks like a very painful manner. I try to fight back a smile at his antics and fail. His attack on me seems like a million years ago. He'd been a monster in my imagination then, now I realize that he's just a sad man with a little bit of power in a world of freaks.

"Come here," the Ringmaster requests, waving me over to the edge of the hill. As I approach, he offers me a pair of binoculars through which he's just been looking. I grab them eagerly. It takes a moment but my eyes adjust to the new perspective as my mentor helps me change the focus.

In the distance, what looks like humongous people stand in stark shadows. The growing warmth of the day makes it look as if heat ripples off the backs of these hunched giants.

"What is it?" I ask, awed.

"New Orleans, our next stop."

As soon as the words leave his lips, I realize my mistake and the giants transform gradually in my vision to the buildings they truly are. I smile at my error and try to make out more details but the city is still too far away. Regardless, I feel shivers run up my spine as I stare at the legendary city of sin and excess.

I'm pulled away from my reverie by the sound of Charlie mocking the still-absent Micky. He's babbling, stuttering, pretending to be the retarded man, spit falling from his mouth, nonsense words flowing from his mouth. An amused audience has gathered and I admit to myself, reluctantly, that he does sound a lot like Micky.

"Where do you think he went?" I ask.

"He's around," the Ringmaster replies, staring out as if he can see the distant city without the binoculars. "Don't let these people fool you. Micky's a lot tougher than they give him credit for. If he's not around, he's probably got a very good reason for it."

"Hm," I reply, moving away from the ledge. "Well, I'm gonna go to the bathroom."

If he hears me, he makes no indication of it.

I move away from Charlie's rapt audience and make my way to the dilapidated wood-paneled outhouse near the side of the road. As I draw closer, its stench reaches me and I hesitate before entering. I can easily swing around back and relieve myself there but the last thing I want is for Charlie to see me from a distance and start making fun of me instead. Taking a deep breath, I push the bathroom door open and enter.

As I stand at the urinal, I can hear Charlie's voice in the background as well as the occasional burst of laughter he elicits from the crowd. As I finish and pointlessly push the broken toilet handle, another sound reaches me from beneath the noise outside: crying. I stop halfway through zipping up my fly and listen, trying to discern the location of the soft weeping. I open each of the stalls, new blasts of stench ballooning out at me from each one, but they're all empty. As Charlie's voice slowly recedes outside and I hear the sound of the truck doors opening, I walk around the perimeter of the bathroom, slowly realizing that the sound is coming from above me. Looking up, I see a small grate that, based on the layout of the structure, can only lead to the women's room.

We've been at the rest stop long enough that everyone has already used the bathroom and I haven't heard anyone enter after I'd made my way in. There are no other cars at the stop, ruling out a civilian.

"Hello? Are you okay?" I call up.

The crying stops for a moment but quickly resumes, only quieter, as if the person is aware of my presence now and trying to hide her own. I wait another minute, hoping the crying will end, but it continues unabated.

I exit the men's room and walk around the small divide that leads to the women's bathroom. I go to push open the door but then think better of it, knocking instead.

"Hello?" I ask again but from here, I can't hear anything, let alone the soft crying. After another moment's hesitation, I finally push forward, entering the much cleaner bathroom, my stomach tightening in potential embarrassment. "Hello?" I try once more, though now it's little more than a nervous croak.

This being my first time in a women's room, I'm surprised initially by the lack of urinals but soon laugh inwardly at my own ignorant mistake. All of the stall doors are closed and the crying is clearly coming from behind one of them. I slowly open each door and hold my breath as I discover them empty, coming at last to the final one against the far wall. Standing in front of it, I can tell now that the crying is definitely coming from within and, with a last unsure breath, I push the unlocked door open.

Micky squats against the wall behind the toilet, his body shoved unbelievably tight into a seemingly too-small space. From my angle in the stall's doorway, it looks as if Micky's top half is actually erupting up and out of the toilet bowl, like some kind of comedic giant who's been half-flushed and is now stuck in an unbearable position. His trumpet and bag lay on the ground next to him.

"Micky?" I say quietly.

His head suddenly snaps up as if he hadn't noticed my entrance and his crying stops abruptly. He stares at me like I'm a complete stranger for a minute and then his eyes clear and a slight smile crosses his face.

"Daniel?"

"Hey, man, you okay?" I ask, taking a step closer to him.

He pushes himself against the wall as if trying to keep away from me but there's nowhere else for him to go. I take another step and say his name again, which seems to calm him. As I draw closer, a horrible smell invades my nostrils and I have to keep myself from gagging. Breathing through my mouth, I grab Micky by the elbow and lift, hoping he'll make an effort, too, because it's doubtful I can get him up on my own. Luckily, he pushes himself against the wall and is on his feet almost immediately. Looking him up and down, I realize where the smell is coming from. Shit stains run up and down both of his pant legs as well as both sides of his crotch.

"I'm sorry," he says, bursting out into tears again.

"No, it's okay, Micky, it's totally okay. Everyone's done that," I lie, but his tears continue to flow.

We stand facing each other for a moment, awkward, and then I surprise myself by leaning forward and wrapping my arms around him in a clumsy attempt at making him feel better. After another minute, I feel his arms wrap around me, too, and his head settles on my shoulder. I breathe through my mouth and wonder if anyone else is looking for us yet.

At length, we disengage and I step away, a bit embarrassed now, and tell him we should probably join the others. I turn away from him and exit the stall and I'm about to leave the bathroom when a sound stops me in my tracks: a trumpet note, clear as any I've ever heard, and mournful. I step back to the stall door and see Micky, now seated on the toilet behind which he'd just been hiding, the trumpet pressed against his lips, a quiet song evolving from that single note, an unknown song of such beauty and sadness that I can't help but smile and want to weep at the same time. I lean against the sink and just listen as Micky plays. His eyes are closed the entire time.

A knock at the door draws my attention away from the song and Micky lets the last note fade. I walk to the door and find the Ringmaster there when I open it.

"I guess you found him," he says, a slight grin forming on his face.

"We'll be right out. Can you grab an extra pair of Micky's pants and bring them back here without anyone knowing?"

He looks at me for a moment, confused, but then nods, not knowing or not needing to know, and heads back the way he came. I walk back to the stall where Micky is now standing, rummaging through his bag, the trumpet once again strewn haphazardly on the floor.

"I didn't know you could actually play that thing," I say, impressed. In response, he withdraws his laughably huge set of keys and then, with his free hand, reaches out and takes hold of mine, peeling back the fingers to reveal my palm. I'm convinced he's about to give me his set of useless keys as a reward for finding him or for not telling anyone about him shitting himself or maybe both, but instead he drops the keys into the toilet with a mischievous grin on his face. Still holding my hand, he leans over and picks up some dirt from the ground and rubs it into my palm. I try to pull my hand back, grossed out by the thought of the bathroom floor muck, but he's stronger than he looks and holds on like a vise. He then bends over and spits into my palm, the dirt and spittle mixing instantaneously. He places two of his fingers against my hand and begins rubbing the mix deeper into my skin, creating a thin sheen of mud that bleeds into the lines of my palm. Micky throws his bag over his shoulder and grabs his trumpet from the ground, then wraps his free hand around my dirtied one. Somehow, the stench is gone now and, standing in the women's bathroom at a rest-stop off a Louisiana highway, we hold hands and wait for the Ringmaster to return with a clean pair of pants.

CIRCLE NINE
THE TRAITOR

CANTO THIRTY-TWO

No one expects a massive ice storm in New Orleans during the summer but it hits the city with a vengeance. The forecast had called for 80-degree weather with scattered clouds. Instead, icy rain descends from a slate-grey sky, slicking roads and causing people to run from bar to bar, the lure of beads not quite enough to expose bare flesh to the elements.

I awake on the morning of opening day shivering and can see my breath as it curls out in front of me. Rushing across the trailer, I notice that the Ringmaster isn't here as I head into the bathroom. I ready myself to pee, my entire body shaking, and almost let loose with a torrent of piss when I realize that the water in the toilet bowl is frozen over. I laugh in disbelief, holding the urine back with two clenched fingers, until the pain becomes too much. Looking around, I quickly shuffle over and relieve myself in the sink, satisfaction outweighing any guilt.

The hot water isn't working either so I get dressed hurriedly, throwing a baseball hat over my bed head, and exit the trailer, and wishing I'd thought to bring winter clothes when I ran away from home. Outside, everyone is out and about, like usual, but the weather has dampened the usual chatter and opening day cheer. As I pass a couple of the performers, I overhear that the show has sold out but they wonder if people will show up in this kind of freak cold front. I make my way deeper among the performers and watch as the workmen struggle to plunge the thick wooden spikes into the frozen ground.

I'm about to ask someone where the Ringmaster is when I see Kane approaching me from his trailer. I'm not sure if he's actually coming for me but something about the look in his eye coupled with how cold I am causes me to panic. I turn and sprint away. The shell of the big top is up so I sneak inside as stealthily as possible. The bleachers haven't been constructed yet so I settle for a bale of hay as a makeshift seat. I sit there for several moments, shivering in silence, when I hear a faint moan behind me. At first I don't see anyone, and then I realize that Charlie is lying on the ground, asleep or unconscious I'm not sure, an empty bottle of Southern Comfort next to him, half-covered in straw. I approach his slightly shaking body and feel pity wash over me as I realize that there are frozen tears on and around his closed eyes. I wonder if someone covered him with hay or if he crawled in here after the big top's frame was constructed in order to be alone. Smiling at him, my first real enemy in the circus, I'm about to walk away and perhaps find a blanket for him when I notice something on the far side of his body. Circling around to the left, I slowly realize that it's Micky's trumpet, or what's left of it, horribly mangled and mutilated.

Pity is replaced by rage as I stare at the trumpet, then at Charlie's puffy, drunken face, then back at the trumpet. Without realizing what I'm doing, I draw back my leg and kick him in the stomach as hard as I can. Charlie's eyes flutter and I step back, ready for a fight, but he merely mumbles something incomprehensible and turns over. I fight an urge to kick him again.

Exiting back into the rain, I set my jaw against the cold and hope this isn't a harbinger of things to come in the Big Easy.

As the night roils across the sky, the rain slowly dissipates and then ceases altogether. The cold grows sharper though, more biting, and long, foreboding icicles grow down from every angle. Despite the freezing temperatures, the audience appears on time, speaking loudly, laughter billowing out in white clouds from their expectant mouths, entering the freak show corridor with an enthusiasm that surprises me.

Someone has managed to restore a modicum of hot water so I pull myself away from the crowd and return to my trailer, hoping a quick shower before the show will rid me of the growing chill in my bones.

Later, as I step outside into the harsh temperature, the crowd buzzes loudly across the clearing from within the big top. Everywhere I look, colorful prisms shoot out through the ice, creating a surreal illuminated path straight to the circus. Excited, I leap off the top step and hurry on my way.

Entering the corridor, I'm reminded of the first time I did so, months ago in Boston, though it feels like years, if not decades. I wonder how my family is; wonder if they miss me, or if they've moved on. For the first few weeks after I ran away, I got a sense from the Ringmaster that the cops and maybe even the FBI were gung ho about finding me, but it's been ages since I've overheard any mention of it. Maybe they all just assume I'm dead.

A pang of guilt washes over me, raising goose bumps on my arm, and I suddenly feel bad for my family, for how hard this must have been for them. But then memories of violence and shame and disgust sweep over the guilt and I shake off the cold, moving forward among the freaks. With the Tattooed Man holed up in his trailer, the Fat Lady still recovering from giving birth, and Hairy Carrie dead, the Snake Charmer is one of the few freaks left in the corridor. She smiles and winks at me as I pass.

I find myself standing in front of Alicia's empty case and place my hand on the glass. To my surprise, it's warm. I whisper her name and ready myself to enter the big top, which has grown hushed in anticipation. With the audience already inside, the Trickster has abandoned his post, a relief considering everything that's happened. But that's when I think I feel the Geek's eyes burning a hole in the back of my head.

I turn, prepared to see his blood-streaked face or a headless chicken carcass in his vein-addled fist, but nothing could prepare me for what I actually see.

The Geek's case is empty.

Well, not quite empty. There are two chickens inside, somehow spared from the Geek's vengeful teeth. But rather than celebrating their survival, the larger chicken is following the other one maliciously, poking at the back of its rival's neck, deep red blood pouring down the back of the less fortunate animal. I stare at this odd spectacle for a long moment as the aggressive chicken continues to attack, digging a hole deeper and deeper into its enemy's neck, the blood spurting freely now.

And it's at that moment that the sound of someone screaming from within the big top shocks me from my reverie and pulls me directly into the center of Hell on Earth.

CANTO THIRTY-THREE

I burst into the big top assuming an audience member has fallen down the stairs or that a child has been scared by the Clowns or possibly even by the Ringmaster himself. But as I take in the scene before me, an unnatural hush having asserted itself within the tent, I stare in disgust and fear at what is actually happening.

In the center ring, one of the bears, Ugolino I think Mal named it, has ripped open Kane's stomach with its now-bloody claws and is feasting on the dying Strong Man's innards. I instinctually begin to move forward to somehow help him but the Ringmaster stands nearby with fear etched on his face. He warns me off with his eyes. The audience sits transfixed, as if hypnotized or too afraid to risk the berserk bear's wrath.

As the light drains from Kane's eyes, I notice a figure dancing around the big top, insane giggles emanating from his red-stained lips. It's the Geek and this is the first time I've ever seen him outside of his case. When he sees me, his laughter increases and I'm unable to suppress a shudder. The Ringmaster's urgent stare instructs me to leave immediately but whatever's keeping the audience and the performers within the big top also keeps me rooted to the spot.

As the Ringmaster opens his mouth to address the unsettled audience or perhaps to call Mal in with his tranquilizer gun, the Geek suddenly changes course and skips into the middle of the center ring. The bear looks up at his approach and pulls its gory maw away from the Strong Man's corpse. I cringe and wait for the enraged animal to rip the emaciated freak to pieces but instead it stares at the Geek with what seems obvious respect. The Ringmaster and his performers, including Mal, who has just appeared from his side-tent, watch in shock as the Geek places his bony hand on the bear's head. A low, playful rumble escapes from the animal's throat. The blood on its fur is in sharp contrast to the red, white, and blue pom-poms on its costume.

The Geek nods at the bear and the creature shambles toward me. I slowly move aside as it stops where I'd just been standing near the entrance and turns, surveying the havoc it just wreaked, apparently standing sentry now. The Ringmaster takes this opportunity to cautiously step forward and approach the Geek, who stares at his boss as if he's been waiting his entire life for this confrontation.

The Geek smiles as the Ringmaster covers the Freak's face in the shadow of his top hat.

"Lou, Stop. Whatever it is you're doing, however you're doing it, stop. Right now."

For a moment, it looks like the Geek's eyes are glazing over and I see smug smiles spreading across the faces of the performers, thinking that their leader, love him or hate him, has just saved their lives. Instead, the Geek's eyes become clear and he giggles silently, nods, and all hell breaks loose.

The lions suddenly roar, startling everyone, and turn on the Lion Tamer, Chuck, and Ness, gutting them instantaneously, claws rending flesh, faces ripped to bloody pulps even as the men are still screaming and trying to get away. The monkeys appears from nowhere, dropping from the rafters, leaping up from the dirt, and attack the audience, ripping women's hair from their scalps, gouging out men's eyes, but strangely leaving the children untouched. Elephants run rampant, breaking easily from any restraints, chasing down Gerry and his fellow midgets, and crushing them beneath their cracked, vengeful hooves. Mal's dogs roam in a deadly pack and slowly stalk the Fire Eater, who backs away fearfully, attempting to fend his attackers off with bursts of flame. As the smell of burnt animal hair mixes with the scent of blood and gore, the dogs, several of which are now on fire, tackle the Fire Eater and literally tear him limb from fiery limb. One of his severed, burning arms lands in a pile of hay, igniting a small fire that grows quickly.

Screaming from above reaches my ears and I stare up and watch as birds of all kinds, creatures that have nothing to do with the circus or its acts whatsoever, attack the Acrobats. They fight off the birds as best they can but, one by one, the Acrobats lose their balance or grip and plummet to their deaths below. Not one of them screams on the way down. Across the big top, I can make out Mr. Atlantis's glass water coffin but can't see him inside it. Blood oozes into the water from his unseen body.

The audience finally reacts, screaming hysterically, pushing past the monkeys where possible, searching for any conceivable exit. The bear by the entrance flap shreds any adult dumb enough to attempt an escape the conventional way. I make my way around the chaos, trying to find the Ringmaster and failing. One of the audience members pushes past me, her nails scraping inadvertently across my neck, reopening the wound from my first attempt at shaving. The blood flows down my chest.

Continuing on, I watch in horror as a half-dozen horses run down and trample the dancers and riders, none of whom I've ever really gotten to know. A few of them survive the initial stomping, calling out to me feebly to help, but the horses hear their weak cries, too, and return to finish the job, blood and brains and guts exploding out across their hooves. The Fortune Teller sits on the first row of the bleachers, her eyes closed tightly, and she barely reacts when a gorilla approaches her, puts its beefy fingers gently on her face, and proceeds to snap her neck. She crumples soundlessly to the ground, her billowing robe covering her face, fingers twitching and then stilling forever.

I move on in fear, circling the big top, moving to the left and attempting to avoid the murderous wrath of the animals. I try, and fail, to help the performers as they're slaughtered one-by-one. The smoke increases and I move farther into the center of the rings, stopping in terror as I realize I'm staring at the top half of one of the female Clowns; the other half is a bloody pulp within an alligator's mouth. The two other female Clowns pull at their sister's arms, even though she's clearly dead. A pair of other alligators approaches them silently from behind and before I have a chance to call out, they attack, wrapping their sharp teeth around the Clowns' legs, the sound of bones breaking the last thing I hear before turning away and hurrying on, fighting to keep from throwing up.

The polar bear, whose ill temper ensured that it was only brought out when performances were going particularly poorly, is feasting on Pietro's shoulder. The old Clown is already dead and has a disconcerting look of contentment on his face. Some of his colorful makeup has rubbed off onto the polar bear's fur, which might have been cute or funny under different circumstances.

The smoke continues to thicken and I suddenly find myself alone, surrounded by screams of agony and the moist, un-nerving sound of flesh being ripped from bones. A pair of figures slowly takes form in front of me and I move forward cautiously, hoping one of them is the Ringmaster.

Instead, I find myself staring at Mal's kneeling form, which is being bitten and clawed by an enraged lion, the same one he saved me from a week earlier in Mobile. Mal sees me approaching, as does the lion, and the animal pulls away from its master, intestines trailing from its mouth, which seems to be upturned in an obscene and impossible smile. Mal collapses to his side but keeps his eyes on me. I look from him to the lion, hoping that the Animal Trainer will somehow save me once again or at least command the lion not to attack but, instead, with his dying breath, he says to me, "Don't let anyone hurt her."

The lion tenses, ready to finish the job she hadn't had a chance to complete in Alabama, when a form divorces itself from the smoke. It's the Geek, and he fixes his yellow eyes on me and then on the lion. He shakes his head at the animal and after a moment, the lion lowers its head and stalks away, a growl of disappointment accompanying its exit.

I cough violently as the Geek approaches and I recoil in fear as he raises his skinny fingers to my face. But he grabs me with his other hand, stronger than I imagined possible, and stares into my eyes. His breath is putrid. Finally, he caresses my face gently and then abruptly lets me go, dancing off into the growing smoke.

I stumble away and realize that everyone I come across is either dying or dead. The animals continue to skulk about but, even when they stare at me with hatred or anger, they move away as if the Geek has silently labeled me off-limits.

My circuitous wanderings fail to lead me to an exit. Instead, I eventually end up in the center ring and nearly trip over the Geek, who's now splayed on the ground, staring up at the canvas roof, his chest oddly still. As I touch the Geek's cold, dead skin, the sound of a gun discharging literally makes me jump. Through the haze of smoke, I can see the outlines of uniformed police officers, who begin firing their weapons with wild abandon at the rampaging animals. I know I should get out of here to avoid being shot but I can't pull myself away from the corpse of the Geek. I suddenly hear something above me and look up, unintentionally following the unseeing gaze of the Geek. The birds that had attacked the Acrobats a few minutes earlier now peck and bat frenetically at the big top's canvas roof. Within seconds, they've managed to create a hole large enough through which they can escape. Although it's stopped raining, freezing cold water trickles down from where it has collected, and falls down onto the Geek's face.

I sit there and watch the ice-water collect and freeze over the freak's eyes as the animals he had so mysteriously commanded are shot and killed around me.

CANTO THIRTY-FOUR

"On march the banners of the King of Hell," the Ringmaster says when he finds me standing over the Geek's corpse.

"Is it over?" I ask, though the absence of guns firing has already answered my question. He nods and I notice that his top hat is missing. Blood runs from a cut on his forehead. My own blood has stopped flowing but I hurt all over. The Ringmaster stares at the ice-covered body on the ground and shakes his head.

"I thought all along that I was in control," he says, barely a whisper, "and I was wrong. So very wrong. I'm sorry I dragged you into this, Daniel."

I try to tell him that it isn't his fault but the words freeze in my throat. Instead, we walk away from the Traitor and step outside. Cop cars and fire trucks are everywhere. The fire's been put out but the big top still smolders. Dawn is just beginning to break, which seems impossible to me. It's Sunday. A strong wind pushes against us as we survey the damage. For the first time, I see tears welling up in the Ringmaster's eyes.

"It's all wrong," he says. "Backward. Upside down. This isn't how it was supposed to happen."

At that moment, three police officers approach us, two of whom hold handcuffed men: the Circus Manager, Charlie, and its Owner, Peter Alpe. Both men wear looks of extreme shame.

The unencumbered cop, his nametag reading Sergeant Jude, steps closer and stares at the Ringmaster with unconcealed hatred.

"I can only guess with that lame fucking outfit that you're the Ringmaster of this shitty little circus."

"You guess correctly," my mentor replies, wiping the blood from his forehead and straightening his tux in an attempt to remain dignified. "And I take full responsibility for everything. You can let those two men go. They had nothing to do with this whatsoever."

Sergeant Jude laughs contemptuously. "I don't think so. You're all going to jail and you'll probably be facing multiple manslaughter charges. Put your hands behind your head, freak show. You have the right to remain silent—"

"Seriously," the Ringmaster interrupts as Jude cuffs him. "It's entirely my fault. I intentionally starved the animals to save money. These men—"

"Enough!" the cop yells, grabbing the Ringmaster roughly by his hair. My mentor clenches his teeth and responds with a sharp intake of breath.

"Leave him alone!" I yell, pushing Jude. All three officers laugh.

"What do we have here?" the Sergeant says, letting the Ringmaster go and wrapping his hands roughly around my shoulders. "Where are your parents, kid? Are you here with them?"

"Fuck you!" I spit. "I work here!"

They continue to laugh at me.

"That true?" Jude asks the Ringmaster. "You hiring little kids illegally? I'd love to slap another charge on you, freak show."

I begin to protest but the Ringmaster silences me for a final time with his eyes. We stare at each other and I realize that he's saying goodbye. I shake my head in silent protest as he responds to the officer.

"This is the kid that went missing a few months ago. I kidnapped him in Boston when he got separated from his parents. I've been keeping him with us against his will."

"Holy shit, it is him," one of the cops says.

"No, he's lying!" I scream but Sergeant Jude pushes me aside. "No, no, no," I protest as the cops lead the three men away. The

Ringmaster looks back, a remorseful smile appearing on his face and just as quickly vanishing. Charlie, Peter, and my mentor are shoved into the back of a police car and the two officers disperse into the growing crowd of cops, firefighters, reporters, and rubberneckers.

"No," I whisper as Jude returns to me. He beckons a female cop over.

"Keep an eye on this kid. He's the one everyone's been looking for."

"Understood," she says, placing her arm gently on my shoulder.

I watch as Sergeant Jude walks away from us and gets into his car and grabs his two-way. Slowly, the other cop car pulls away and I watch in silence as the Ringmaster disappears from my life, his last act one of betrayal and sacrifice, until all I can see is his dark hair in the back of the receding car, and then he is gone.

After a few moments, the female officer begins leading me toward an ambulance, asking me my name, assuring me that everything's gonna be okay now, that I'll be with my family soon.

As I sit in the back of the ambulance, surrounded by the remnants of the circus, I find myself looking up and staring into the distant sky, where the rising sun's light has yet to reach. Smoke still billows out from what remains of the big top and it somehow causes the distant stars to shine even brighter before succumbing to the insistent glow of day. I sit there for what seems like ages, just watching the pulsing pinpricks of light, thinking of the Ringmaster and of Alicia and then of her estranged twin sister, Beatrice, who I hope someday to find, and a smile reluctantly spreads across my battered face.

As I wait to be returned to a life I had so willingly abandoned, I close my eyes and, in the expansive confines of my mind, walk with my friends one last time beneath the stars.

ABOUT THE AUTHOR

Brendan Deneen has been a professional comic book writer since 2006, when his critically-acclaimed series SCAT-TERBRAIN was released. Since then, he has worked on FLASH GORDON, CASPER THE FRIENDLY GHOST, and many others, including the upcoming RUDOLPH THE RED-NOSED REINDEER: THE ISLAND OF MISFIT TOYS original graphic novel. THE NINTH CIRCLE is his debut prose novel.

Follow Brendan at:
http://www.facebook.com/brendan.deneen